CHRISTMAS BLUES

Leigh Jarrett

Published by Steambath Press

Paperback published November 2019
ISBN-13: 978-1-927553-49-7

Chapter One

Summer wasn't finished with us yet. The sunbaked blacktop beneath my feet, pungent from the heat, radiated a steady, scorching warmth up my body as I crossed the street. It was mid-September, and my position as the job site safety inspector for Hollins Construction had brought me to Denver, Colorado, more than forty minutes outside my usual region of Boulder.

The resident inspector in Denver had taken his family on holiday to Europe, leaving me struggling to cover both his and my territory.

I rolled up the damp sleeves of my white, button-up shirt as I made my way toward a coffee shop down the road from my last inspection of the day. My shirt had started the day clean and crisply ironed, but now it was rumpled and sticking to the small of my back. The clothing we were required to wear as *professionals* entering construction sites was insanely inappropriate for the current weather. We'd been sweltering in high-eighty-degree heat for weeks.

The handle of the coffee shop's door felt cooler than the surrounding air as I gripped it and pulled it open. I was welcomed by a gust of what felt like an arctic breeze, in contrast to the air outside. I took a deep breath of it, inhaling relief from the heat and a pleasant assault of freshly brewed coffee and cinnamon buns.

If I didn't have other commitments, there was every chance I wouldn't leave this coffee shop any time soon. I looked back across the street at my car. I'd left the inspection reports I needed to complete by the end of the day lying on the passenger seat.

Later.

I'd head back out to the car to retrieve them once my body had cooled enough to brave the heat again.

The young, pink-haired woman behind the counter caught my attention by clearing her throat and greeting me as *Sir*. I'd reached the front of the line, but my mind had wandered. I was thinking about the long drive home to Longmont, realizing it would be late by the time I arrived.

I'd need to call my sister and ask her to pick up the kids from the after-school babysitter's—again. She wouldn't be pleased. She'd picked them up twice already this week. Luckily, today was Friday, meaning I'd be home for the next two days, relieving my sister, Janice, of her Auntie duties—favors actually... in other words, her continual saving of my ass.

I perused the board of coffee options and decided on something cold.

"Mocha Frappuccino, please," I said as I opened my wallet and peered inside, not sure if I should use my debit or credit card. I had no idea how much money was in my bank account. The kids had needed new clothes and a ridiculous amount of school supplies for *back to school* last month. Taylor, my eldest son, aged eleven, had been the most troublesome in the clothes shopping mayhem. He'd insisted the other two, Cindy aged eight, and Marcus aged five be left at home—with my sister while I'd taken Taylor out on his own.

Thankfully, she'd agreed ...again.

"Your name?" The bubbly female voice tugged me away

from my wandering mind again.

"Sorry. It's Ryan." I removed the solitary credit card from my wallet. I didn't like using it for anything other than business expenses, but there was no sense in taking the risk of having my debit card declined. I'd never been this short of money before, aside from my college years. But everything was different now. I had mortgage payments, medical insurance, orthodontics, baseball, karate, ballet lessons—and a ton of other expenses to cover. Being a parent was expensive, and without my wife's income, I was struggling.

I wandered to the end of the counter to wait for the barista to complete what I hoped would be a drink capable of chilling my insides, matching the gradual cooling of my skin.

"Ryan?" A voice behind me had me turning around. I wasn't sure if I'd misheard my name being called. I didn't know anyone this far from home, and I didn't recognize the scruffy, dark blond-haired man approaching me; the cosmopolitan style of his clothing threw me off even further. Bare feet in white sneakers, torn couture jeans with a silver wallet chain, a black and white striped shirt, and a tailored suit jacket. He looked like a rock star.

People didn't typically dress like that in Denver.

"Ryan Middleton?" The man reached out to shake my hand, grinning as if greeting a lifelong friend, his unkempt beard accentuating his lips launching to speak before I'd had an opportunity to reply. "What are the chances? I haven't seen you since …I was like, what …thirteen? I just moved back here last week, and here you are."

He clapped his hands together after releasing my reluctant grip. I had no idea who this guy was. The handshake had been awkward, but he'd persisted undeterred. "Did you move out this way?" he continued. "I thought for sure you'd stay in Longmont.

You never struck me as a big city guy. What about your parents? I sure miss them ...Bill and Evelyn. Your mom was always such a riot." He sighed and laughed softly, shaking his head. "Sam and I used to drive her insane."

A drop of ice-cold condensation ran down my arm from where I was holding my plastic cup full of reprieve from the heat. The straw had yet to find its way to my mouth. How could this guy possibly know so much about my family when I had no idea who he was?

"I'm sorry, I don't think ...," I stammered.

"Oh man, you have no idea who I am, do you?" His neck flushed red, spreading right the way up to his cheeks. "Of course, you don't. The *aged thirteen* thing since I saw you last...." He extended his hand again. "Michael Sanderson. I was a friend of your brother's."

"Mikey?" I clapped my hand into his, laughing.

I'll be damned.

It was no wonder I didn't recognize him. The annoying, scrawny, pimple-faced teen, the kid who always asked way too many questions, ate all the M&Ms out of the mixed nuts, and borrowed video games out of my room without asking, was standing before me, unrecognizable.

Well, almost unrecognizable. Now that I knew who he was, his animated expression, intense green eyes, and habit of speaking way too fast confirmed his identity. Michael had been my younger brother, Sam's best friend for years. His family had moved away partway through their junior year. I'd been twenty-one at the time, busy at college and all that went with it, reading, studying, ...and spending time with my girlfriend, Rebecca.

I had, however, been sufficiently observant of my brother's feelings. Losing his *partner-in-crime* had hit him hard. He and

Michael had been inseparable since kindergarten.

"What are you doing back here?" I asked. "I didn't think anyone who'd experienced life in New York would decide to move back across the country to *Mile-High City*."

Michael snorted in amusement. "Not entirely my choice… moving back." He motioned toward a table with an open laptop and ceramic coffee cup on its surface. "Do you have a minute to sit? I'd love to catch up."

"Sure, yeah." I followed him to the table and pulled out a chair as Michael closed the lid of his laptop and picked up his coffee. It looked to be of the hot variety. Crazy in this heat. "So, why did you move back here?"

"I really didn't have a choice." Michael set his coffee down. "My ex-wife took a job out this way. We agreed she couldn't pass it up." He pursed his lips. "Well, we *eventually* agreed. She wore me down. We've been divorced for over a year, and she's still making life decisions for me. Next thing I knew, we were moving."

I furrowed my brow. "Okay, so …I don't understand why you followed her?" I finally took a sip of my drink, languishing in the rush of cold descending down my throat.

"For a damned good reason." Michael grinned. "Two reasons, actually. Mandy and Michael Jr, two of the most fantastic, tiny humans on the entire planet. Not being able to see them, watch them grow, go to their baseball games, and attend their school recitals…." He shook his head. "I would move anywhere to be with them."

I released the straw from my mouth and shook the cup to encourage more of the drink to settle near the base of the cup. "I know the feeling. I have three of my own."

"Now that doesn't surprise me." Michael leaned forward

against the table. "I always figured you'd be a family man. Sam and I were constantly in your face, messing with your stuff, deliberately annoying you …but you never lost your temper with us. You were even brave enough to take us places. Like the state fair …do you remember that?"

I nodded my head, grinning. "Yeah, my friends harassed me for weeks about that. But I didn't want you guys to miss out. Not a single one of our parents wanted to take the two of you."

"See, that's what I mean." Michael reclined in his seat and crossed his arms. "So, did you end up marrying Rebecca? Sam said you two were pretty serious ...last I heard from him."

I lowered my gaze then looked away, concentrating my attention on the road running past a nearby window. There was an antique shop directly across. Rebecca had always loved poking around amongst the bits and pieces to be discovered in stores like that.

"Yeah." I looked up at Michael. "Rebecca and I got married after college."

"And you stayed in Longmont?"

I nodded my head, solemnly.

Michael tipped his head to one side, likely contemplating whether he should comment on my obvious discomfort as a result of his question. He chose to change the subject.

"What about Sam? He used to write to me at least once a month, then sometime around grade eleven, he started spouting off about self-sufficiency and his plans to head off into the wilderness to live off the land. Then—nothing. School finished, and I didn't hear from him again." Michael set his hands on his laptop. "He didn't do it, did he?"

I nodded. "Yeah, he did. He took off a few days after graduating high school. He'd been working at an outdoor recreation store for a few years before he left. Saving up money, buying supplies. He even got his hands on a rifle. Loaded everything up one morning ...and left."

"Damn, that's crazy. Not surprising, but crazy. When did you hear from Sam last?"

"Oh, wow, ...um." I scrubbed my hand across my mouth, thinking. "Sixteen months ago, maybe."

Michael's brow creased. "So, you don't even know if he's alive."

"No." I shrugged. "But he's living life on his terms. There's something to be said for that. Although my family doesn't necessarily feel the same way. Especially my mom and Janice."

Michael grinned. "How is that lovely but angry and vindictive little sister of yours?"

"Better. Still angry most of the time, but bearable. Janice is a big help when it comes to the kids. Picking them up. Dropping them off. Watching them overnight." I sighed, gripping my cup tighter in my hand. I hadn't meant to expose the extent to which my sister helped me out.

Michael knew something was up, but he was choosing to set it aside, most likely assuming Rebecca and I were divorced.

"So, what are you doing for work?" Michael seemed perfectly content to press on with new topics of conversation. I was thankful for that. I loved my job. The hours were long, and there was an annoying certainty of arguments between myself and the construction heads, making every day a potential for strife, but I could talk about it for hours. Not that I would, of course. Even though Michael had asked, it would be cruel to subject him to the entire outline of my job.

"I'm a regional safety inspector for Hollins Construction. I drive around and make sure the workers on our construction sites are following proper safety protocols." I smirked. "Sometimes, if I'm lucky, I get to do safety demonstrations."

The blank look on Michael's face told me even that small amount of information had nearly put him to sleep. I drummed my fingers on the table and grinned. "I know. Boring, but I love it."

A half-smile lifted Michael's cheek on one side. "As long as you enjoy it …" He snorted, and a short laugh erupted, sputtering from between his lips. He clamped his hand over his mouth to control it. "I'm so sorry," he said after removing his hand. "Seriously, if you enjoy your job, I'm thrilled for you. Really."

"Ha-ha." I leaned back in my chair. "And what do you do that's so much more exciting?"

"Well," Michael said as he indicated toward the back of the coffee shop with his thumb, "I have a recording studio right next door. I mainly work with new independent artists, but sometimes I get the occasional audiobook or voice-over booking. I'm still new here, so I'll need to build a new base of musicians, but that shouldn't be a problem. I have a good reputation."

I coughed out a short laugh. "Okay, you win. That's way more interesting than what I do."

"Depends on your perspective."

"Um-hm, right."

Michael looked down into his empty cup, then back up at me. "Hey, I only have a few more hours of production work left to do. Would you like to come in and check the place out? Play with the mixing board a little? Order a pizza?"

I looked out toward my car. Checking out a recording studio sounded infinitely more interesting than the paperwork I had to do. I wrinkled my nose and turned back to face Michael. "I'd love to, but I have a lot of paperwork to finish, then I need to drop it off in Boulder before I head home. I'm going to be late as it is."

"That's too bad. Do you come into Denver often? Is it part of your work area …?"

"Not usually. I'm covering for someone." I tapped the tabletop. "How about next Friday?"

"Nah." Michael shook his head. "I have my kids next weekend. I only have them every second weekend, so I try to be finished work early on a Friday. I like to pick them up from school."

"Understandable." I rolled my shirt sleeves down and buttoned the cuffs. The air conditioning was doing an efficient job. A nice change, but heading back into the heat was going to feel dramatically different. Especially since the air conditioning in my car had decided to act up, blustering lukewarm air across my skin, irritating me more than if it hadn't been working at all.

I slipped my phone from my pocket and handed it to Michael. "Give me your number, and maybe we can figure something out."

"Awesome."

Michael typed in his contact information then handed my phone back. I sent him a quick text, so he had my number as well.

Then we stood, gave each other an exuberant handshake, and went our separate ways.

Chapter Two

"Dad! Marcus has been stealing my Halloween candy again!" Taylor came flying into the kitchen, nearly tripping over the open dishwasher door. Taco Tuesday had been chaotic, but as always, worth it. As far as I was concerned, ground beef, salsa, lettuce, cheese, and taco shells covered off every major food group, and the kids loved it. Filling their own taco shells was disastrously messy, and the concept of do-it-yourself food set off more than a few arguments as they fought for control of the toppings, but it was a tradition. A tradition their mother had started. One I had no intention of putting an end to ...ever. Too much stability had been ripped from their young lives already.

"I told you," I said to the heavily furrowed, red, thin-lipped face of my eldest staring up at me, "to put your candy up high where Marcus can't reach it. If you leave it under your bed, it's fair game. To both Marcus and Cindy ...and me."

"You wouldn't touch it."

"Oh, wouldn't I?" I winked at him. "There's this thing called *candy tax*. Payable by all children to the parent or parents who braved the elements and costuming mayhem to take them out trick-or-treating."

"That's not real," Taylor replied with uncertainty. "There's no such thing as *candy tax*."

"Maybe not, but my love of *Snickers* bars is." I ruffled Taylor's hair even though I knew he hated it. Soon my eleven-year-old would become a teenager, and I wouldn't be able to get away with annoying him with stuff like that. Hormones would be raging, and the ugly head of teen angst was apt to explode all over my meticulously spotless kitchen if I tried.

"Dad, don't," Taylor said as he ducked away from my hand, his mop of blond hair falling back in place, barely exposing his eyes. He needed a haircut. I looked at the other two as they leaped and climbed up and over the back of the couch in the attached family room—again and again, screeching with excitement. They all needed haircuts. Yet another thing to add to my ever-growing to-do, money to be spent list.

I closed the dishwasher door and pressed the heel of my hand against my forehead, massaging my brow, hoping to fend off the tension headache building there. I was exhausted.

Not quite done yet.

I picked up the tattered dishcloth, infused it with scalding, hot water from the tap, and set to work on the counters and stovetop, bottle of antibacterial spray in hand. I'd only just finished wiping down the last counter when the sound of the front door opening interrupted my plan to stretch out on the couch and close my eyes. Cindy and Marcus hadn't tired of their latest movie yet, so distracting them for a bit of peace wouldn't have been too much of an issue.

My sister, on the other hand....

"How's my big brother," Janice said as she strolled into my kitchen and opened one of the cupboards. She wasn't looking for an answer, so I leaned against the counter and sighed. One moment of peace was apparently too much to ask for. I knew I shouldn't complain. I really shouldn't. My sister was a lifesaver.

"Wine?" Janice lifted two wine glasses down and swung the fridge open. There was still a bottle of white we'd been working our way through over the weekend. I was more than happy to help her finish it off.

"Please." I took the glass, savoring the cool, delicate surface.

Most of my day, in the drinking glass department, consisted of plastic cups with twisty straws. Marcus loved them, and Cindy insisted on using one because Marcus did. And Taylor.... Taylor had decided he wanted to drink everything out of a plastic sports bottle. Somewhere along the way, I had picked up an old coffee mug and never used anything else.

"Ryan." Janice shoved me, jostling me, then went to sit on a stool on the other side of the kitchen island. "It's only Tuesday, and you look like hell."

"Thanks."

"No, really. You need a break." She set her wine glass down and drummed her fake nails on the marble countertop, the repetitive, rhythmic clicking imitating how I imagined the marching feet of a caterpillar might sound as it moved across the island toward me. I reached forward and set my hand on top of hers to stop her.

"Sorry." She lifted her wineglass and took a long sip, then set it down. "I think you need to get out and do something."

"I get out." I crossed my arms. "I do stuff."

"I'm not talking about driving kids to lessons or going grocery shopping." Janice poised her hand above the countertop, as if she might start click-drumming again, but laid her palm flat on the surface instead. "I'm talking about going out and having fun."

I set my wine glass down and turned toward the sink. "I'm not having this conversation with you again." I gripped the handle of the faucet and turned the water on. Cold then warm. I ran my hands under it, washing them. "I'm not ready to start dating yet." I turned the water off. "You know that." I swiveled back to face her. "Not even Amy in Engineering."

Janice's lips were tight as she nodded at me. "I know." She

took another sip of her wine. "Oh, I have it." She set the glass down and held both hands out, a smile spreading across her face. "Have you talked to Michael since you bumped into him?"

I tipped my head to one side, resulting in a satisfying crunch. I had meant to call Michael, but finding a block of time to hang out with him when I had three kids to deal with was impossible.

"Didn't he invite you to check out his recording studio?" she continued.

I nodded. "Yes, but I can't drive all the way to Denver when I have stuff to do around here." I raised my hand, pointing in the direction of the utility room. "I haven't done laundry in over a week."

Janice placed a hand on her hip, staring me down. "You're going to miss an opportunity to hang out in a recording studio …you—who loves music as much as you do …in order to do laundry?" Then came the finger waggle. During any conversation with Janice, there was an unobjectionable finality in the wings once the finger waggle happened. I didn't stand a chance.

"Hell, no," she said. "*I'll* do your damn laundry if it gets you out of the house. I'll scrub your floors—I'll even clean your windows. Whatever it takes. You're going out, and that's final."

See—final.

"Janice, I can't ask you to …"

"Stop, right there." Janice reached down to the end of the island, grabbed my phone, and pushed it toward me. "Phone him. Right now." She picked up her wine glass. "I'll wait right here until you do."

Damn it, Janice.

I scanned through the numbers on my phone until I found the listing Michael had keyed in.

Mikey.

It made me smile. He'd always hated me calling him Mikey when we were kids. Like really hated it. Chucking X-box controllers at my head, pushing me out through the treehouse door level of hated it. I stared up at the ceiling as his phone kept ringing. Seven, eight …I thought for sure I was going to be directed to his voicemail.

"Hey, Ryan! Oh, man, I'm so glad you called. I've meant to call you, but life kept getting crazy. The kids, the studio. I've got some amazing talent cycling through here. Album after album about to explode onto the music scene in no time. You wouldn't believe some of these young musicians. Damn, talk about scary gifted." A pause followed, which I assumed was for him to take a breath, but it lingered. Nope, …he was waiting for an answer.

"That's awesome." My mind went blank as I fumbled for the additional words to express how happy I was for him. Instead, I had come off sounding flat and disinterested. I stared at Janice. This was her fault. I was too tired to be having a conversation with anyone.

Say something.

"Sounds like you're not having trouble bringing in business," I decided on finally.

"Yeah, it's been good …" Then his voice trailed off into an agonizing silence.

"Mikey …Michael, I'm sorry. I'm flying on empty today. Janice's first words to me when she walked in the door were that I looked like hell." I smiled with relief as a soft laugh carried through the phone. "I'm really excited everything's working out the way you'd hoped with the studio."

"Thanks. Hey, what about you? Any exciting safety demonstrations on your horizon? How not to fall off buildings? Hardhats 101?" A laugh rolled up from my gut, spreading an uncharacteristic grin across my face that had Janice raising an incredulous eyebrow at me. It felt good. "Welding safety for squirrels?" Michael added.

"Stop." I coughed out a snorting laugh then caught my breath. "Squirrels are no longer allowed on the job site. It goes against regulations. Their little fluffy tails kept catching fire, and the tiny welder's masks were too difficult to manufacture." Janice's expression appeared all kinds of confused now. I could see she was contemplating my sanity.

"Ah, see …there you are," Michael said. "I knew you were in there somewhere, mister I'm-too-tired-to-form-a-sentence."

"I just need a break." I turned my back toward Janice and leaned against the counter. It suddenly felt as though she was eavesdropping on a conversation I'd prefer to keep private. "I'd like to head into Denver, take you up on your offer of checking out your recording studio. Is your invitation still good?"

"Always. You're always welcome to drop in." Michael continued speaking, but the volume of his voice changed. He must've put his hand over the microphone, I could hear a muffled conversation in the background, then Michael's voice carried through again. "Sorry. The ex-wife was delivering her marching orders. I'm taking the kids to the babysitter's tomorrow morning."

"What's happening this Friday?" I stuffed my hand into my jeans. "Are the kids staying with you?"

"Nope, it's a daddy-only weekend. You going to head my way? I have a fabulous blues band booked in that'll take you back to that LP collection of yours."

I shook my head, laughing, remembering the number of times Michael had asked to borrow records from my limited teenaged collection. Nothing like what I had now. It was an obsession, collecting LPs. The albums lining the walls of my living room were a testament to that.

"I wouldn't miss it. If I shift a few things around at work, I can head home and change, then be there around five o'clock. Does that work?"

"Perfect. I have to warn you though, the studio is typically a pizza-only dinner zone."

Simply pulling into the parking lot of Michael's recording studio brought my stress level down. The anticipation of hanging out with someone other than my kids, or my sister, all of whom I love, had carried me through a tough week at work. A week that normally would've had me curled up on the sofa before I'd made dinner. In short, it would have been a macaroni and cheese, I don't care where you sit and eat it, daddy is passed out in front of the TV—week.

I switched the engine off and stared at the grey, cinder block building. Michael had instructed me to park around back. A simple, metal door was the only indication anything lay within. A rusted light fixture with chipped, red paint washed the door in dim illumination.

The hallway within was dark at first, but as I moved toward where I hoped I'd find Michael, a series of evenly spaced, bare bulbs affixed to the ceiling above my head lit my passage. Music posters, old and new, began to appear on the walls. I took my time, perusing them, giving each a moment of my attention. I wondered how many of the bands with their glossy, concert venue ads stapled to the walls, Michael had produced albums for. I had to admit, I was proud of the guy.

"Ryan, you made it!" Michael strode down the hall and clapped both hands on my shoulders. "You are not going to believe these guys. Amazing! They remind me of ..." He snapped his fingers a few times in thought. "Albert King and Otis Rush, *Door to Door*. Blew me away. Man, I remember the day you brought that album home. You played it over and over for hours."

Michael chuckled and sighed, then began walking down the hall toward a battered wooden door at the far end. The concrete floor beneath my feet, which extended all the way from the entrance, gave way to worn, 60s era green carpet.

We entered a cramped room, low ceilings, buzzing with electrical equipment. The sparse furnishings consisted of two office chairs, a torn, dingy sofa, and a coffee table straight out of the 70s. Across one wall, beneath an interior window that looked out into a room strewn with musical instruments, microphones, headphones, studio monitors, and a snake-pit of cables, was a lit production board amass in dials and sliders, and digital displays.

I took a step toward it to get a better look.

"It drove Sam mental," Michael continued, "but I couldn't get enough. Hanging out at your house, listening to your music through the walls. That's when I realized music was going to be huge in my life." He set his hand on my shoulder. "I should probably thank you for that."

"Yeah, sure …," I mumbled. I hadn't done anything more than hide out in my room with my high-school sweetheart, Rebecca, listening to music to keep the world at bay. It hadn't even occurred to me that Michael was listening intently to what I was playing. I'd rarely given the geeky kid in my little brother's room much notice unless he was bugging me for something.

I looked around in awe. This world of Michael's was beyond incredible. My initial reaction had caught me off guard. The feel of the place, even the faux-wood paneled walls. This was where great music was preserved for all time. I was effectively speechless.

Michael had left his awkward kid stage far behind.

"Don't tongue-tie yourself telling me what you think," Michael said.

"I'm sorry." I shook my head and turned around to face him. "There's a lot to take in."

Michael sat down in one of the office chairs. "Yeah, I suppose it is overwhelming for anyone who hasn't spent their lives in one of these dungeons." He grinned. "Wouldn't trade it, though."

"I can see why." I sat down beside him, dearly wanting to know what the purpose was for everything on the production board. When the band reentered the recording room after their break, I sat in silence, watching intently as Michael worked his magic.

More than once, I found myself grinning uncontrollably. It was like a dream being there, watching music be produced to perfection. The completed recording of the final compilation for the day left me awestruck. Michael's production skills were epic …for the lack of a better word.

"So …," Michael said after powering everything down and flicking off the lights. I followed him as he led me into what appeared to be a break room, furnished with yet another sofa from a bygone era. "What did you think of the band? Incredible, right? I picked them up after hearing them play in a cruddy, little bar downtown. Convinced them they should produce an album. I've had to absorb a lot of the cost for their studio time, but it's all about marketing, right?"

I sat down on the sofa. "Um, yeah, I guess so. I don't know much about marketing."

"True." Michael sat down beside me, pizza pamphlet in hand, and passed it to me. "Not much call for advertising in the safety squirrel world." A big grin spread across his face. "Last jab, I promise. If it weren't for guys like you, there would be more families suffering because of accidents on job sites. It's important work."

My mouth lifted in a half-smile, not sure if he was being earnest or joking around. Michael seemed serious enough. "Thanks," I replied. " I appreciate that."

"No worries." Michael stood and headed for a small fridge. "Sorry, the guys weren't able to stick around for you to meet them."

"That's all right." I shrugged. "Maybe next time."

"So, there will be a next time, hey?"

"Are you kidding? Watching you in there was incredible."

"Glad you liked it." Michael grinned at me over his shoulder. "So, food. Can you pick the pizza? I'm pretty easy."

I flipped open the pizza pamphlet. "What? You stopped hating pineapple?"

Michael turned around, two beers in hand. "No …yuck. Anything but that." He popped the cap off my beer and handed the icy bottle to me. "I'm surprised you remember."

"Are you kidding me? You used to make a little pile of pineapple at the edge of your plate and start flicking them at Sam when my mom's back was turned."

I smiled. "I remember because Rebecca used to get furious when they landed in her lap."

I lowered my head, staring at the floor. "But that was a long time ago." I could hear Michael exhale deeply beside me.

He was holding his tongue again.

Eventually, I would have to tell him what happened to the love of my life, my best friend, and the caring, intelligent mother of my children. Just not today.

Michael placed his hand on my shoulder. "And there's no need to talk about it. I have no intention of prying ...especially on an empty stomach." Michael released me and took a swig of his beer. "Choose already, would you. I haven't eaten since breakfast."

Huddled on the sofa, laughing and reminiscing, the time passed quicker than I thought possible, considering Michael was my little brother's friend for all those years, not mine. Our eight-year age difference had relegated Michael to the outermost edge of my attention sphere.

Not so much anymore.

Michael's easy, exuberant manner had captured my full attention.

"That's quite the schedule of extra-curriculars." Michael licked the smear of pizza sauce from his thumb and reached for his beer. "Mandy and Michael Jr. are both in soccer. Other than that, they spend most of their time running around out in the yard with one of us. Soccer, baseball ...trampoline. I'm sure Mandy would love something like karate."

Michael set his beer on the table. "I can't imagine how that would go over with her brother. We'd have to enroll them both. But then they'd be practicing on each other every spare moment they had, which would likely result in a few hospital visits. Mandy is a tough little thing."

"I hear you. I used to feel sorry for Cindy because she's sandwiched in between two boys." I shook my head. "I needn't have worried. She's more than capable of holding her own against those two." I toyed with grabbing another beer but decided against it. I had a long drive home. One beer was my limit when I knew I'd be driving. I was the only parent my kids had left. I wasn't about to risk ripping that away from them for the sake of my throat feeling a bit dry.

"When the weather sucks," Michael added, "all the craft materials come out. Both my kids love making stuff. My ex-wife's house looks like an art gallery run by preschoolers."

Michael smiled, and I felt compelled to smile along with him. His pursuit of full participation in his kids' lives warmed me through. He was a great dad. A great guy, really.

"My kids too. The messier and more hellish to clean up, the better." I grinned, laughing. "Wouldn't trade them and their perpetual mess for the world."

Michael closed the pizza box's lid then looked over at me, his eyes wide with excitement. "We should get them all together. Have a crafting extravaganza."

"Thanksgiving theme?"

"Perfect." Michael slapped a hand on my back and rose to his feet. "I'll hit the craft store and round up as much orange, brown, and yellow paper as I can find." He clapped his hands together. "And feathers …and googly eyes for the turkeys."

I found myself laughing aloud, long and hard, something I hadn't done in a very long time. "Since you seem to have the art project ideas well in hand, I'll leave you to it." I stood and retrieved my coat from a row of hooks lining a large section of the wall. "Let's do it at my place. I have glue and pipe cleaners, and probably whatever else we might need."

"Glitter?"

I nearly snorted, my grin already demonstrating the breadth of my amusement at the idea of two grown men getting excited about the details of making paper turkey ornaments.

"Yes, we have glitter," I said. "Plenty of it, all colors."

"Perfect. Mandy loves her some bling encrusted turkey

décor." Michael reached out to shake my hand and gripped it tight in his own. "Let's try for next weekend. Check your calendar and text me. When it comes to activities for the kids, I can make almost any day work."

When I reached my car, I stopped and looked over at Michael waving to me from the doorway of his studio. What were the chances? Running into someone from my past who embodied two of my core values—a passion for *The Blues* and a couple of kids he was willing to do anything for.

"Hey," I shouted as I reached out to open my door. "We should catch a Broncos' game sometime."

"Boo-hiss." Michael laughed. "Giants rule."

"Traitor."

I grinned as I slipped into my car, laughing to myself.

Ah, well. Nobody's perfect.

I waved at Michael through the windshield as I backed away from the building.

Chapter Three

The doorbell rang the moment I finished taping the plastic, dollar store tablecloth I used for crafts, in place. The multi-colored surface of stars conjoined by a rainbow of paint smears and paste had been abused by months of use, but it was still capable of doing its job. My grandmother's antique dining table was safe from the messy rigors of family life.

"Is that them?" Cindy shrieked as she flew into the front foyer, clapping. She'd been up most of the night, beyond excitement at the idea of meeting new kids.

I had to admit, I was looking forward to the creative chaos Michael and I had planned. We'd made a few phone calls back and forth, confirming we had everything we needed to make this a memorable day for the kids.

"Yes, go ahead," I said to Cindy. "Open the door."

Her little fingers struggled with the deadbolt until it clicked. She hauled on the doorknob and threw the door open, sending the handle crashing into the wall, denting the sheetrock.

I rolled my eyes. Yet another repair job.

Michael laughed in commiseration as he stepped into our old Victorian house, which was in desperate need of a paint job. His daughter, Mandy, took one look at Cindy and tore off into the family room with her. Michael Jr., in contrast, was gripping tightly to Michael's leg, reluctantly being dragged along as Michael took a few more steps into the foyer.

"Hey," I clapped my hand onto Michael's shoulder then squatted down to be eye level with Michael Jr. Aside from the lack of dark blond facial hair, Michael Jr. was a miniature version of his dad, right down to those thick, dark lashes framing his brilliant green eyes.

"Your dad tells me you love dinosaurs. Is that true?" I asked.

Michael Jr. scowled at me but nodded his head, yes.

"Marcus," I shouted toward the family room. "Could you go upstairs and gather up all your dinos? You have a visitor who would love to see them."

Marcus poked his head around the corner, peering at Michael Jr.

"Please," I said. "You two can practice naming them."

"Or make them fight?" Marcus asked as he wandered toward us, arms crossed. Five years old, and he was already well on his way to mastering the art of parent manipulation.

I rose to my feet and looked at Michael for input. I wasn't sure what level of roughhousing Michael Jr. was used to. He was only four.

Michael shrugged. "As long as it's just the dinosaurs fighting. Don't be beating each other senseless with them." He grinned as the two boys wandered toward the stairs together.

"And watch the spikey bits," I added as they reached the top of the stairs. "I don't want to be patching up puncture wounds on either of you."

"Yes, Dad," Marcus whispered as he stepped into the upstairs hallway.

"That's them dealt with for the time being," I said, leading Michael toward the kitchen. "Can I offer you something to drink?"

Michael slid onto one of the barstools facing the kitchen and dropped the load of bags he'd been carrying onto the floor at his feet. "I'd normally be begging for a beer after that drive, but I suspect I'll need my wits about me once the crafting gets underway."

"Rambunctious journey?"

"You have no idea." Michael looked up at me, grinning. "Okay, yeah, …you do." He nodded his head when I lifted a bottle of iced tea from the fridge for him. "Mandy likes her window open. Michael Jr. wants it closed. He likes the radio on. Mandy doesn't …unless she's allowed to sing. Which Michael Jr. hates." He took a swallow of iced tea. "Two pee breaks …one for each." He set the bottle down. "Oh, and I brought along the absolute *wrong* video. Mandy hates *Princess Ponies* now. I swear it was only yesterday when she loved them."

"Stuff like that changes quick. I've taken to writing it all down."

"I'll have to start doing that."

I looked out toward the dining room table. Most of the supplies I needed were in my grandmother's old mahogany sideboard. Not it's intended use, but it suited my purposes. Art and homework supplies in one place next to where the kids used them. Having them at hand saved me from running around the house looking for stuff. An adjustment I'd had to make once Rebecca wasn't able to get around easily anymore. Doing art with the kids had become her greatest joy.

Michael obviously approved, chuckling and patting the top of the sideboard as I started unloading the baskets of construction paper, tissue paper, egg cartons, and pipe cleaners, and tins of crayons, felts, pencil crayons, glue, scissors …and glitter.

"Handy," Michael said as he began spreading the supplies out on the table so everyone could reach everything. "My apartment isn't set up well for the kids yet. We've been concentrating on my ex-wife's house, making sure it feels like home for them."

"You'll get there."

Taylor slumped into a seat at the table. "What lame thing are you making us do this time?"

"And this is what you have to look forward to." I placed my hand on Taylor's head, warranting me a scowl. "Michael, this is my son Taylor."

"Hey, Taylor." Michael extended his fist, and Taylor bumped his knuckles against it. I could tell my son was marginally impressed; a glimmer of admiration lit up his eyes. Michael with his torn jeans, black lace-up boots, leather jacket, and flashy rings—so much cooler than his own dad.

"Dad says you own a record company?"

"A recording studio. I help musicians record their music. Their managers take it from there."

"Are you famous?"

Michael smirked. "In some circles, I suppose."

"Wow, really?"

I smiled. *So* much cooler than dear old dad.

Taylor picked through some of the supplies on the table and looked up at Michael. "Are you going to help with this Thanksgiving stuff?"

"That's the plan."

"Okay," Taylor said, then sighed. "Then I guess I'll make something."

As Taylor ran off back toward the family room, Michael leaned up against me, laughing. "I'm sorry, your kid is priceless."

"Just wait until you have one his age. You won't be laughing."

Michael stepped back. "Oh, come on. Teenagers are a riot. I wasn't so bad."

I snorted out a laugh. "Are you kidding me? You were such a pain in my ass." I rubbed my hand across my mouth, then imitated knocking on a door. "Ryan …Ryan, are you in there? I can hear you. I know you're in there. Ryan …Ryan, we just want to borrow …" I snorted again, the corners of my eyes tearing up as an infectious grin spread across Michael's face.

"…an extra Nintendo controller," Michael chimed in, in his best teenaged boy voice, cracking, rasping, and squeaking. "Your Tetris cartridge …Super Mario Brothers, SimCity, Donkey Kong." He slammed his hand on the table, laughing. "No, wait, Donkey Kong was Sam's."

"And then you wanted to borrow every new record I picked up." I gave Michael a friendly shove. "John Lee Hooker, Robert Cray …Robben Ford. It was constant."

"Good thing you were nice enough to lend those to me." Michael crossed his arms, his expression softening. "I wouldn't be where I am today if you hadn't indulged me."

I shook my head. "Come on. That's not true. You have a love for the blues. You would've found your way there eventually."

Michael sighed. "Maybe." He jerked his thumb in the direction of the living room. It lay directly off the front entry and was typically unused in everyday life.

I grinned. I knew what Michael had spotted in there.

"That is quite the record collection you have out there."

"It's a weakness of mine. I had to build the floor to ceiling shelving to house them all."

Michael whistled and shook his head. "What you've created in there is nothing short of an art installment. Any chance I can peruse through it later?"

"Just like old times?"

Michael snorted out a laugh. "Exactly."

Cindy ran up and grabbed me around the waist. "Can we start now?"

"Are we ready for this?" Michael said as he cocked his head to one side.

I nodded. "Heaven have mercy on us."

The fallout was precisely as bad as I imagined, although Michael and I managed to contain most of the glitter and glue to the table. The kids were content with what they had made, and the fridge and dining room wall were now decorated with abstract renditions of turkeys, pumpkins, and something Michael and I agreed was supposed to be a *Horn of Plenty*.

"Did the beeper thing go off? Is the oven heated?" I turned toward the stove, chicken strips placed evenly on a baking sheet, ready to be baked. Crafting had run long, and the troops were hungry. A dinner of chicken strips, fries, and a veggie platter had received the most votes.

"Hard to tell amid the din of war cries." Michael laughed and opened the oven door. "Feels hot enough. Let's chance our arms on this one. We can always cut them open to check if they're done." He closed the oven door after I placed the tray on the rack. "We have a few kids to spare. If we lose a couple, it'll effectively serve to quiet things down around here."

"True." I placed my hand on the fridge door. "I'm cracking open a beer. It's either that or lie down for a nap." I looked over at Michael. He looked as frazzled as I felt. "Do you want one?"

Michael shook his head. "I can't. I have a long drive ahead of me. Once we feed these kids, I'm going to pack them into the car and head home."

My chest tightened. I was enjoying the comradery of having someone to share the burden of wrangling the kids into some semblance of obedience and calm. The thought of being left on my own again unsettled me. It had been almost four years since

Rebecca left us. It felt good to have an extra set of hands, even though the number of kids had increased from my three to five.

"Hey," I said, thinking aloud. "Do you think your kids would be up for a sleepover?"

Michael's eyebrows arched dramatically, accentuating the intense eye contact he always maintained when speaking to you. "You want us ...all of us to stay overnight?"

"Might be fun."

"Might cause me to have an aneurism." Michael pointed toward the fridge. "Beer."

"Is that a yes? I have a guest room upstairs, and we have sleeping bags kicking around somewhere, so your kids can easily bunk up with mine."

Michael exhaled as he opened the beer, I'd handed to him. "Let's do it. Sanity be damned."

Four hours later, the calm was palpable. The kids had been tucked into bed; stories read ...multiple times by both of us. Sips of water had. Monsters chased from beneath beds and closets. Night lights adjusted. Last-minute trips to the washroom completed.

Now it was quiet. The only sound, the stylings of Brownie McGee, the ice in the bottom of my scotch glass, the crackling of the burning logs in the fireplace, and the relaxed exhalations of my beleaguered comrade.

"This is nice." Michael lifted his feet and placed them on the coffee table in front of the armchair he'd melted into once I'd handed him his drink.

"One of my favorite times of the day."

"You're a brave man."

I set my glass on the side table. "How so?"

"Doing this on your own." Michael took a sip of his drink,

not releasing me from his gaze. "I don't want to pry, but …" He pointed toward the shrine-like collection of photographs of my wife on the fireplace mantel. "I couldn't help but notice. Either you're pining for a woman who has chosen to cast your family aside, or something else happened."

I could feel the lines settle across my forehead. It had been horrific. The diagnosis …the decision to refuse treatment, but Rebecca had insisted Marcus' life came first.

"Rebecca …" I looked down at the carpet, then brought my hands together. I rubbed my fingers around the wedding ring I still wore on my finger. "She was diagnosed with breast cancer six years ago." I released a steady breath to try to calm myself. "She was pregnant with Marcus at the time. She chose to refuse treatment until after he was born."

Michael leaned forward in his seat, reaching for, but not quite making contact with my arm. "I'm so sorry, Ryan."

I looked up at him, the sincerity emanating from Michael's eyes washed over me, warm and comforting. There had always been a kindness about Michael.

I rotated my glass atop the coaster on the side table, a thin, watery ring forming there. I lifted the glass to my lips and finished the finger I'd poured myself.

"Once Marcus was born, Rebecca started treatment. But it was too late. Her cancer had metastasized. She was riddled with it. Her lymph nodes, lungs …everything."

Michael rose from his chair and came to sit beside me. He didn't launch into a stream of commentary and questions, but set himself to listen instead. I was opening up to him, and he had chosen to respect that and just let me talk.

"Rebecca died when Marcus was two. It was two years of agony for the entire family. Trips back and forth to the hospital.

Care nurses in and out of the house at all hours. And Rebecca... by the end, she didn't even look like herself. She'd shrunk away to nothing in front of our eyes."

"Shit," Michael whispered beneath his breath. "I can't imagine what that would've been like, watching the woman you love slip away."

I grabbed my glass and headed for the kitchen. "It certainly made me appreciate the people in my life. The kids. My parents, Sam ...my sister."

"It sounds like your sister has really stepped up."

"Yeah, Janice has been a saint." I dumped the ice cubes from my drink into the sink, rinsed the glass, and set it aside. I'd done enough dishes for one night. "Hard to believe, I know."

Michael leaned against the counter beside me. "And Sam?"

I shook my head. "He had no idea what was happening. He didn't descend from the bush until six months after Rebecca died." I wiped my hands off on the tea towel hanging down the side of the lower cabinets. It would need to go in the wash soon. "He took off again as soon as he heard."

"I'm sorry." Michael set his hand on my shoulder.

"It's not your fault. Sam's personality is all about avoidance of stressors in everyday life."

"No, not that." Michael gave my shoulder a squeeze, sending a tendril of heat up through the muscles to my neck. I closed my eyes to soak in the sensation. It had been a long time since anyone other than my kids and family had touched me.

I longed to bask in that feeling for a while longer.

Michael released me and crossed the kitchen. "I meant, I'm sorry I wasn't here for you. If I had known ...if Sam had told me, I would've come out for the funeral at least."

"Thanks." I scrubbed my hand across my face. I was

exhausted. I looked up at Michael and smiled. "I appreciate you saying that."

Michael stared down at the floor. "I guess it would've been strange, your little brother's irritating, elementary school friend showing up out of nowhere."

I smirked. "You weren't that irritating."

"Hah." Michael left the kitchen, headed for the stairs. The sound of someone crying had caught his attention. "You're a terrible liar."

I lay in bed, staring up at the ceiling. Downstairs I could hear Michael orchestrating the task of preparing breakfast. He seemed to have it well in hand, giving me a few minutes to think about my life, something I rarely had a chance to do. My chance encounter with Michael had been so incredibly unexpected; both the meeting and the friendship we seemed to be cultivating.

I hadn't had anyone I could call a friend since my wife, Rebecca. I'd never been overly social. I had a few acquaintances at work. One, in particular, Amy, but she was looking for more than friendship. Something I wasn't ready for yet.

I lay my arm across my eyes to keep the sun from intruding on my thoughts. I might never be ready. Sure, I liked Amy. She was intelligent, funny, and beautiful, but that didn't mean I should ask her out, no matter how often my sister suggested it. Amy had never been married, and she didn't have children. She couldn't possibly understand what my life looked like and how little time I would inevitably have to spend with her. The schematics weren't long-term relationship friendly.

"Ryan!" I could hear Michael making his way up the stairs. The smell of bacon, and what I hoped was coffee, wafted through the doorway as he opened the door. He stood there looking at me.

"Up." He waved a spatula at me. "No breakfast in bed during circus hours. If you want some food, get your ass downstairs before the kids eat everything."

A stupid grin spread across my face. The guy was a riot. And he got it. Michael understood what it was like being a parent, even if he didn't do it full time like me. He was fully committed to those kids and knew how to manage them like a pro.

I watched him standing in the doorway, his expression expectant, his spatula at the ready, looking as though he was prepared to smack me with it if I didn't get up. Maybe this was exactly what I needed. A good friend. Not a girlfriend. Just someone to hang out with who understood where I was coming from, someone I had a bit of history with. I didn't have to hide my daily struggles from Michael. I could be myself. His presence put me at ease.

And that was something I desperately needed in my life.

"All right, all right." I sat up and looked around for my jeans, not entirely sure where I'd tossed them the night before. "I'll be right down."

"Excellent." Michael smirked at me. "Just a heads up, I may have made a slight mess of your immaculate kitchen. I let the kids help. Taylor was a bit careless when he was using the electric beaters in the pancake batter. I managed to get most of it off the walls …the ceiling not so much."

He turned to leave then turned back, barely able to contain his amusement as the grin I'd been wearing slipped from my face. Maybe I'd been hasty in my assessment of his parenting skills.

"You are so predictable," Michael said then turned back into the hall. "Your kitchen is fine," he shouted over his shoulder. "Except for the scorch marks from the bacon incident."

I could hear Michael snickering as he descended the stairs.

A surge of solidarity and calm dragged me back into the bedding, satiating a need for companionship I hadn't known the full depth of until now.

Having Michael as a friend was going to be good for me.

As reported, the kitchen was fine. More than fine. Michael was the kind of guy who cleaned as he cooked. The only fallout, a mixing bowl, beaters, and a spatula.

I headed for the coffee. Michael had dug out my French press, a glass and chrome miracle that made even the cheapest of coffees taste better. It had been a wedding present from Rebecca's cousin. Now it acted as a reminder of our lazy Sunday mornings together.

I hadn't touched it since she'd died.

Michael couldn't have known.

I filled my cup with the dark roasted, revival elixir, and headed to the fridge for some milk. "You know how to put on quite a spread." The grill was still hot, and Michael was moving between it and the small frying pan he was using for the eggs.

"I don't mind cooking. It keeps my hands busy while I work through the next day's musical arrangements in my head." He nudged me with his elbow. "Which reminds me. I haven't put any music on yet. The kids had me up before I'd had a chance to scan through your collection."

I set my hand on Michael's shoulder. "That I can do. Cooking is merely a necessary evil in my eyes." I was reluctant to break contact with him, allowing my hand to linger for a moment.

"Music," Michael reminded me, his eyes studying me as I released him.

I ran my fingers along the protective plastic sleeves on my albums, until I found the section I was looking for. Robin

Trower's *Bridge of Sighs* was soon gracing the living room and beyond. Not a blues classic by any stretch, but my musical taste had expanded somewhat over the years.

I turned it up louder than I usually would have, Michael's loud exclamation of, "Sweet!" from the kitchen encouraging me. Walking back to the dining room and seeing the kids dancing around to the music, sticky maple syrup hands and all, elicited an unexpected sigh of contentment.

Our house seemed happier than it had in a long time.

"Eggs, Ryan. Sunnyside up or over easy."

"Over easy, thanks."

Michael winked at me. "Two over easy coming right up."

"Can I do anything?" I figured I should at least offer to help.

"Mm ..." Michael turned around, a piece of bacon bobbing about between his lips as he tried to eat it hands-free. He crunched the last section between his teeth and licked his lips. The action left them rosy and glistening in sharp contrast to the dark blond, bristly appearance of his beard; the refined line between it and his jawline blurred with shadows of overnight growth.

I smirked at him. In addition to his beard's rugged look, Michael's hair was tousled, sticking out in every direction, his eyes alight with amusement at the look I was giving him. Even his bare feet, padding about the kitchen, so incredibly white in contrast to his black jeans made me smile. The guy was comfortable in his own skin, confident. I admired that.

"What?" Michael made a stupid face at me, then went back to cooking my eggs. "Fill up my coffee for me, would you. No milk, no sugar."

"You're brave drinking my no-name coffee without disguising it."

"Better than instant, so I'm happy." Michael slipped my eggs onto a plate with a stack of pancakes and three strips of bacon. It was more food than I'd seen for breakfast in a long time.

"This is awesome, thank you."

"Hey, it all came out of your fridge. I just made it edible."

I refilled Michael's coffee cup and carried my food through to the dining room. I managed to find a place that wasn't too sticky with breakfast residue. The kids were in the bathroom down the hall, washing up. I could hear Taylor ordering them around.

"Hot water, soap …now dry them. Next!"

Michael sat down across from me.

"Sounds like Taylor is enjoying being in charge."

"As long as he doesn't traumatize your kids. They're not used to getting barked at by an older brother." I cut my egg into pieces and used a wedge of pancake to scoop it up. *Beautiful*. Food always tasted better when someone else made it. "He's growing up so fast."

Michael mumbled a response around a mouthful of food then burst out laughing, covering his mouth to keep anything from falling onto his plate.

My eyebrows rose in amusement, and I set my knife and fork down at the edge of the plate while Michael caught his breath.

"Oh, my god," Michael exclaimed at last. "I'm sorry. The way you said that …he's growing up *so* fast. You sounded like my gramps back when I was a kid."

I tossed a small crumb of bacon at Michael's head. "Are you calling me old?"

"The tone. It was in the tone." Michael brushed a hand across his hair, dislodging the crumb. "And the words." He rose to his feet. "And the old man body language."

Michael grinned, scooting past me into the kitchen before I could retaliate.

I leaned back in my chair. "Is there enough coffee for another?"

"Nope, but I can make some."

"You don't need to do that." I shoveled the rest of the food into my mouth, collected up my plate and cutlery, and headed for the sink. "I can make some later. Right now, I want to—"

"...get these dishes washed," Michael chimed in.

I snorted, laughing. "You are such an ass."

"Guilty." Michael's voice echoed as he crossed the tiled front entry. "I'm going to snoop through your LP collection. I'll set some aside I'd like to borrow."

A wide grin spread across my face as Michael took off into the living room.

Some things never change.

Chapter Four

The kids were in bed. It was dark, it was late—and it was November twelfth. The night four years ago when my Rebecca took her last breath.

I slumped into the corner of the sofa; my third whiskey reduced to water and ice. Janice had offered to take the kids for the night, as she did every year, but like every other year, I'd refused.

Taylor, Cindy, and Marcus were the last remaining link to my wife. I needed them around me as I wrestled my way through the shadows of a beautiful life cut short.

I set my glass on a coaster and heaved myself to my feet, headed for the bottle of Jameson I'd left on the counter in the kitchen. Halfway there, overcome with anguish, I crumpled to my knees, the tears I'd stoically contained all day falling, emboldened by waves of gut punishing gasps.

I rolled toward the cupboard, not caring if it supported me. It wouldn't be the first time I'd ended up on the floor in a heap.

The pummeling weight. The loss of my heart—my angel, was staggering.

I slammed my fist into the fridge door.

Damn her.

Four years without hearing Rebecca's voice, seeing her smile. Four years of not spending each night snuggled up with her reading the children their bedtime stories.

Four years of arriving at soccer games, ballet recitals, and martial arts exams without the woman I loved by my side.

Four years of details gradually fading. The sound of Rebecca's laugh, the scent of her skin—the feel of her fingertips stroking my face, all drifting like delicate threads on the wind.

I cupped my hands over my face and closed my eyes, willing my mind to produce even a millisecond of one of those senses. Very little rose to the surface. Even the few sweaters of Rebecca's I'd insisted on keeping had long since lost their aromatic connection with her.

I dug in my pocket and pulled out my phone. It was one in the morning, much later than I'd realized. I used the counter to pull myself up and took the bottle of whiskey with me back to the family room. Sitting on the floor in front of the entertainment center, I began fishing through the family movies, prepared to tear myself open further by watching our wedding videos.

As I slumped forward, my head came to rest against the stack of videos I'd pulled out, and my phone slipped from my hand onto the floor.

Michael.

I need Michael.

I don't know where the urge came from, but it gripped steadfast to my mind, unrelenting in its insistence. Michael was the only one who could talk me through this, ease my pain.

I retrieved my phone and scrolled through the contacts until I arrived at *Mikey*. I released a sigh, pinching the bridge of my nose as I pressed *call*. A wave of embarrassment and regret for bothering him so late heated my face as a drowsy, scratchy voice answered.

"Ryan? Is everything all right?"

I froze, realizing I wouldn't be able to contain my emotions if I began to speak. The best I could articulate was a whispered,

"No."

Michael's tone changed, his voice losing its sleepy quality. I could hear sheets rustling in the background. "What's wrong? Did something happen? Are the kids all right?"

"Rebecca," was all I managed to say before the sobbing erupted again, stifling my ability to elaborate further.

"Rebecca? Oh, god, is this the day she passed away?"

I could hear the clink of a belt buckle as Michael's muffled voice broke through the convulsing racket I was making. My puffing exhalation of air must have been confirmation enough.

"I'll be right there," Michael said, sounding fully awake now.

Before I had a chance to object, Michael had disconnected our call.

Some forty minutes later, there was a quiet knock on the door. I'd tried phoning Michael to tell him not to drive all the way here. That it was too late. That all I'd wanted to do was have him at the other end of the line. That the smooth, rolling sound of his voice would be enough to comfort me.

My hesitancy fell away as soon as I opened the door and saw Michael standing there. His look of profound concern nearly crippled me. Michael cared deeply for me. He'd driven all this way without a moment of pause. It was more than I ever would have expected from him.

But it was precisely what I needed.

"Dammit, Ryan." Michael gathered me into his arms, securing me against him as if I might slip away. "Why didn't you tell me when I was here this weekend? I would've been here for you."

"I couldn't ...," I choked out as I clung to him, succumbing to his compelling embrace. Michael's warm hands, one on my neck, one on my back, easing my desperation.

His grasp became tighter, then released, then closer still—created an enveloping reprieve from the pain. I tucked my face into the crook of his neck, inhaling the scent of stale cologne and perspiration, and hung on to him far longer than I'd intended.

Michael took a step back and grasped both my shoulders. "Let's go inside. It's freezing out here." He guided me back into the house and closed the door behind us. It was only then that I realized Michael was wearing his slippers. He'd rushed out of his place to be here for me.

"You didn't have to come all this way for me."

"Don't be ridiculous." Stepping into the family room, Michael picked up the glass I'd been using and the bottle of Jameson and took them into the kitchen. "Go sit down."

I obeyed his instruction, somewhat, perching myself on the arm of the family room sofa. I could hear Michael tidying away the evidence of tonight's drinking spree. Then a rush of water from the tap and the click of the kettle being flicked on. "I'm making you some tea."

"Okay," I mumbled, not even sure if he'd heard me.

Michael sat down beside me as I crawled back into my spot on the sofa.

"You've become one of my best friends, Ryan," Michael said as he leaned forward, hands clasped, supporting himself on his knees. "This is what friends do. We're here for each other." He glanced over at me. "You don't have to go through stuff like this on your own."

I nodded, feigning acceptance, but the fact remained... "I didn't want to bother you."

"You're not a bother. Ever." Michael patted my knee then stood to go deal with the tea he was making. "You need to believe me when I say that."

I did believe him. The sincerity in Michael's voice spoke of a man who would never lie to me.

Michael set a cup of tea on the table beside me and resettled himself at my side. The weight of his body on the cushions caused me to lean into him.

Instead of adjusting myself to move away, I decided to stay where I was, enjoying the dependable, steady feel of his body against mine.

I picked up my cup and sipped at the green tea Michael had made. I looked over when he nudged me, his open hand extended toward me, two aspirins resting there.

"I suspect you're going to need these," Michael said as he placed them in my hand. He was right. I'd drunk enough to cause myself significant grief as the hours wore on.

I set the pills on the table beside my tea. I'd wait until it cooled, then take them.

"Thank you," I said, lowering my chin toward my chest, exhausted. I turned my head to look at him. "Thank you for everything. Coming here tonight …your friendship. Everything."

Michael nodded. "Anytime." An awkward silence followed until Michael looked up and saw the stack of videos sitting on the entertainment center. "What are those?"

I released a long, anxious breath. "Wedding videos."

"Oh." Michael rose to his feet and started looking through them. "Was the plan to reminisce or torture yourself by watching these."

I shrugged. "A little bit of both."

"You're not laying any guilt on yourself about Rebecca's death, are you?"

"Not really, no. It was her body. Her choice."

"And what about Marcus?"

My brow wrinkled. "I try not to think about that. It's not his fault, but sometimes ..."

Michael came back to sit beside me as I leaned forward, my face in my hands. It tore at me. There were moments I toyed with the *what-ifs*. What if Rebecca hadn't been pregnant with Marcus? What if Rebecca had chosen to save her own life instead of that of our unborn child?

"It's all right." Michael's arm slipped around my shoulders and pulled me to him. "It's only natural to wonder if things could've turned out different."

I hadn't needed to say a word. Michael knew where my mind had gone. I should've felt embarrassed, but I didn't. Not around Michael. I sensed it wasn't in his nature to judge.

I let my head recline backward onto his arm, and he hugged me tight against him. Those same tendrils of heat I'd experienced with him before returned tenfold.

I stroked the wedding ring on my finger. "I miss her so much."

"I know." Michael's cheek came to rest on my head, his free hand seeking the one I'd just placed on his chest. I gripped tight to his hand, indulging in the warmth of his skin.

Maybe it was the amount of alcohol I'd consumed, but for a moment, I considered snuggling into Michael, closing my eyes, and letting the steady rise and fall of his chest lull me to sleep.

"Ryan ..." A body shifted beside me. I opened my eyes and immediately regretted it. The sunlight streaming in through the family room windows sent streaks of pain straight through to the back of eye sockets. I grabbed my aching, spinning head, and sat up, disoriented.

"Did I fall asleep?"

"Snoring like a bulldozer in two seconds flat." Michael's chest shook as he laughed. "I was going to wake you and escort you to bed but decided against it. I was comfortable enough, and I figured falling asleep a second time might not come as easily for you."

"You stayed here on the sofa with me all night?" My face flushed with the realization I had curled up against Michael after all. I clambered to my feet—too fast. I grabbed for the arm of the sofa as the room turned into a tilt-a-whirl.

"Whoa, careful." Michael's strong, firm hand grasped my elbow, steadying me.

"I'm fine." I stumbled forward, using the walls—anything to ease my way to the stairs. I needed my bed. Work wouldn't be expecting me. I always took the day after Rebecca's death off.

Taylor and Cindy.

School.

Michael must've sensed my alarm. "Don't worry. Janice showed up around seven-thirty, woke Taylor and Cindy up, fed them, and drove them to school. We had a terse, whispered conversation."

"That must've been awkward."

"With you snoring and drooling all over my chest... yeah, kind of."

"I don't drool."

Michael laughed and pointed to the dark spot on his sweater. Okay, now I was embarrassed ...and I needed to throw up. I was going to need Michael's assistance for a while longer.

"Can you check on Marcus?"

"On it." Michael took the first couple of steps to the landing with ease. Without question. Without clarification. Without a moment's thought for himself.

"Wait." I grabbed the post at the bottom of the staircase. "I'm keeping you from work."

Michael grinned at me. "Seeing the look on your sister's face when she saw me sitting there holding you is worth more than any amount of work I might get done today."

Oh, God.

Janice was never going to let me live this down.

Janice wasn't finding this amusing. Walking in and finding me sound asleep on some guy she didn't know had rattled her. Michael had, of course, immediately introduced himself, but doing so hadn't had the desired effect in appeasing her.

"The kids saw you like that," Janice said as she played with her keys while we stood in the front entry. She was spinning them around and around on her finger, nauseating me further. I tore my attention away from tracking them.

Michael had left around eleven, and Janice had doubled back after running some errands. In that amount of time, she'd managed to work herself into a high level of annoyance with me.

"And?" I crossed my arms. I wasn't in the mood for a lecture from my baby sister.

"And they shouldn't have seen their dad curled up on the sofa with some guy, drunk."

"Michael isn't some guy, he's Uncle Mike, and I doubt they cared."

Janice scowled at me. "Cindy asked me if Uncle Mike was your boyfriend."

"Well, I hope you set her straight." I stormed off toward the kitchen, Janice following hot on my ass. The sight of the two clean teacups set carefully in the drying rack took me back to the night before. I turned to face her. "Michael was here when I needed him."

"You could have called me."

"I know." I looked down at the floor, brushing my foot across a dented tile in the vinyl flooring. The entire floor needed to be replaced. "It's different, though, hanging with him." I smiled as I met her eyes. "Guy stuff, you know. He gets me."

Janice crossed her arms, pursing her lips in contemplation before speaking. "I hadn't realized the two of you had become so close."

"Well, there you go then. Now you know."

My head began swimming a whole new series of strokes, threatening to expel the dry toast Michael had made me this morning onto the floor. "Janice, can we discuss this later." *Or preferably not.* "I need to lie down before I fall over."

"Do you need me to pick the kids up from school?"

"I'll be fine by then." I offered her an unconvincing smile. "Thanks, Janice."

I held the front door open as she stepped out onto the front step. The fresh, cold air blowing past my face eased the pounding of my head, somewhat. Perhaps I could take Marcus to the park before we picked the other two up from school.

Right now, though—bed.

Marcus could curl up with me and watch videos on the TV in my bedroom.

I stared at the last text message from Michael. *"Call me when things quiet down."* The time stamp on the message said *9:37 pm*, which surprised me. I'd expected Michael to have crashed from exhaustion by now. Earlier in the day, I'd asked him if he'd managed to get any sleep last night with my dead weight plastered to his chest.

He'd answered *no*, but not to worry about it.

That he hadn't minded.

I was starting to think Michael's friendship was more than I deserved.

My favorite cup tumbled out of my hands onto the kitchen counter, bouncing once before coming to rest uninjured on its side. I'd been fumbling with things all day—words and objects.

Not because I was hungover, but because I was distracted.

Waking up in Michael's arms this morning had messed with my head.

The kettle stopped hissing as I lifted it off the stove then poured the hot water into my cup, now full of hot chocolate powder. I dug through the utensil drawer, found the small whisk, and set to work mixing. And thinking—again. All day, I'd kept telling myself it had been natural to seek solace in someone last night, and Michael had been there to provide me with that.

Nothing more.

Except, it felt like more.

I tapped the whisk on the edge of my cup, set it in the sink, and stared out the window into the darkness. I'd been drunk last night, but not drunk enough to miss the fact Michael and I had stepped over a line in the *strictly-guy-friends* etiquette handbook.

Sure, I'd been distraught, but we'd both sought more contact than strictly necessary. I wasn't sure what to make of that, other than it had felt good.

I rubbed my thumb along the smooth surface of my wedding ring, remembering Michael's intimate embrace. It had been a long time since someone held me like that.

That's why I hadn't pulled away.

It was as simple as that.

Retrieving my hot chocolate from the counter, I headed for the stairs and the refuge of my bedroom. The kids, after a disorganized dinner and movie, hadn't given me much fuss when it came to bedtime. I think it was apparent, even to them, that daddy wasn't feeling well.

After that, I'd fallen asleep on the sofa—wishing I wasn't alone on it. A few hours had passed, but not enough to stop me from following Michael's message to call him.

I flopped down on the bed and pulled the quilt Rebecca had made over my cold feet. She'd agonized over every little detail of that quilt, stitching together perfect little blue, pink, and yellow squares. It had been her first and last quilting project. Not because of the cancer, but because I'd suggested to her that the kids might be too young to hear the kind of language that tended to stream unfiltered from her mouth as she struggled to piece together the blocks of material.

Michael picked up after one ring.

"Hey, Ryan. How are you feeling?"

"I've been better. I maxed out the number of aspirin I'm allowed to take in a day hours ago. And the children were worried I might be dying."

Michael's whispered response of, "That must've been scary for them, considering," barely traveled through the phone.

I ran my hand across my face. For a split second, I'd forgotten the anniversary of Rebecca's death had been yesterday. "Fuck," I whispered as I pulled the quilt up to my chest.

"It's all right," Michael replied. "You're bound to slip up sometimes."

"I know, but that's not the worst of it." I reached for my cocoa. "I'm beginning to lose track of things about her. Little things. But things I never thought would slip away from me."

"Like what?"

I took a sip of my cocoa and set the cup back on my bedside table. It was too hot. "She sometimes sang to the kids before bed. The same songs, again and again." I touched the rim of the cup as I attempted to recall the memory. "It's gone, Michael. I have lain here night after night trying to remember the sound of her voice as she sang those songs."

"But, you're able to easily recall the memory of her singing to the kids."

I nodded, even though he wasn't there to see. "That's something I'll never forget."

"Maybe you should try concentrating on the memory of the emotion invoked rather than beating yourself up for letting some of the finer details go. It might bring you some peace."

"Maybe. I'll try. I might even be able to sleep."

"I could always drive out and let you drool on me some more."

"Ha. Ha." I smiled as I lifted my cup to my lips. My cocoa was a better temperature now.

"I'm serious. I would do that for you." Michael's voice sounded sincere, with only a hint of humor. A part of me wanted to call him on it, ask him to come out.

Which meant it was time to change the subject.

"Hey, your ex, Brenda, you said she's a real estate lawyer?"

"Yeah, are you thinking of selling? She knows quite a few realtors."

"God, no. Not unless I'm forced to. This is the only house the kids have ever known." I drained my cup and set it aside. "I just thought your ex might know Janice's husband, Jim Crawford. He's a big real estate guy. Keeps Janice living the life she always dreamed of."

"Brave guy. Do they have any kids?"

"Not yet, no."

"She seems to have taken to yours. Her Auntie Bear teeth came out large when she saw me on the sofa with you. Not sure what she thought was happening. Maybe she thought I was a burglar who'd broken into your house and somehow lured you into falling asleep on me."

"No, she figured out who you were pretty quick. She was taken aback because she hadn't realized how close we'd become …being that your Sam's kindergarten friend and all." I snorted through a laugh. "When Cindy saw us, she asked Janice if *Uncle Mike* was my boyfriend."

A hearty laugh rumbled through the phone. "Jeez …kids. They kill me."

"Right?"

"So, when do you want to hang out next?"

The question warmed me through. I missed having Michael around already. We hadn't had much time to talk last night before I'd passed out. And this morning …this morning had seen me running back and forth to the bathroom while Michael entertained Marcus.

"I'm not sure," I replied as I closed my eyes, listening for the sound of Michael's steady, rhythmic breath. *There it was.* I focused on his exhalations, recalling the feel of his arms holding me firmly against him as I nestled into his side.

"Ryan? Buddy? Are you falling asleep?"

"Mm …maybe." I switched my bedside light off and slid down in bed. If I hadn't been so tired, I would've been alarmed by the thoughts racing through my mind as I drifted off.

Chapter Five

I pulled into Denver's Inspiration Point parking lot and shut off the engine of my Cherokee. It had been Rebecca's, but it was running better than the Chrysler rust bucket I'd been hauling my ass around in for years. Scanning the other cars in the lot, I spotted Michael leaning up against what looked to be a brand new Mercedes SUV.

That bastard.

I laughed to myself, locked the doors, and waved at Michael as I crossed the parking lot. We'd agreed to meet at the park, head up to the lookout, then load ourselves into Michael's car and take in the sights. It had been a last-minute arrangement. Janice had, during our usual Saturday morning coffee, offered to watch the kids for the day, and I had jumped at the chance to head to Denver.

It was a strange sensation, arriving at a park kid-less. The last eleven years of my life had been dedicated to my kids. Rarely did I do something for myself.

"Hey," Michael shouted to me. "How are you doing?"

"Excellent." I reached for Michael's outstretched hand and came in for a typical bumping shoulders guy hug, nothing like the one he'd endued me with a few nights ago. The memory of which was still confusing my senses. I pointed at his car. "Nice ride."

"Yeah. It gets me places."

I nodded my head. "Looks like the weather might hold for

us."

"Yeah, it got kind of messy yesterday."

I smirked and looked at the sky. From embracing on the sofa to talking about the weather in three days flat. Funny how that works. "Well, I'm glad things aren't awkward between us."

Michael snorted out a laugh. "I was just going to say that."

"Glad we got that out of the way." I shoved Michael as we headed for the trailhead and took off at a jog. He eventually caught up, pushed me back, and put me in a headlock, laughing as he rubbed my head. When he finally released me, we were both gasping for breath.

It felt good to have our friendship back on track without any weirdness lingering between us. I'd been concerned. Crossing that line on the sofa had unnerved me upon reflection.

It didn't matter now. It was a beautiful morning, and I wanted to reach the lookout before the weather decided to change on us. The city had received a dump of snow last night, the mountains even more so. Inspiration Point was one of the best places to see the extended range thrusting upward from the primarily flat landscape of Denver.

Rebecca and I had often walked up there in the summer, blanket in tow, to watch the sunset. Another reason I loved the place. It was ripe with memories.

I took a deep breath, gazing out at the scenery.

I needed to start looking forward.

The scenic path stretched out before us, still covered in a dusting of snow, pine trees guiding our way. A smile played on my lips as I glanced over at Michael. The wind was gusting toward us, messing up his hair. His nose and cheeks were already responding to the cold, pinking up and making him appear more rugged than he usually did. It was a good look on him.

Michael laughed. "What are you looking at?"

I hadn't realized I'd been staring. He'd caught me from the corner of his eye. Now the full force of Michael's stunning, inquisitive eyes were on me.

I shook my head. "Nothing."

"Wait, no ..." Michael grabbed my arm, bringing us to a stop. "What?"

"It's nothing." I shrugged. "It's just, you look so different from when you were a kid. I was trying to find you in there."

Michael took a step toward me, his eyes drawing me in. "I'm right here, Ryan." He tugged at my sleeve. "You don't have to keep looking."

I couldn't tear my attention away.

His eyes had captured me.

"Maybe I want to," I whispered.

"Then I suppose I'll be forced to push you off the lookout." Michael gave me a playful shove, then grabbed hold of me. He placed his hand on my chest and stepped into my personal space.

I held tight to the sleeve of his coat. "Or not ..."

"Yeah, maybe not ..."

I could feel Michael's breath on my lips, the scent of the peppermint gum he was chewing filling the space between us.

Then, without cause, the moment came to an end.

We parted, and I stood there, dumbfounded, as Michael challenged me to race him. I had no idea what had just happened. I'd practically invited him to push the boundary of our friendship.

And he'd accepted.

I wasn't sure what, if anything, I should take away from that.

I ran to catch up with Michael, walking silently by his side until we arrived at the lookout. I found a spot, and Michael took a seat beside me, braving the cold ground for a moment, so we could relax and look out over the view. The sun had decided to play in our favor.

The snow-peaked, craggy mountains were living up to their reputation. The color contrast and starkness of them in the distance made the city below seem inconsequential in the scheme of things. Our time on the planet was finite in comparison.

"It's beautiful," Michael said, looking over at me.

"Yeah." I leaned against him, reveling in Michael's response as he pressed his shoulder to mine. It was impossible to decipher what my mind was trying to accomplish.

All I knew was I needed to be near him. Sitting here, so close to Michael, I was tempted to increase the stakes and reach for his hand.

I closed my eyes instead.

You're losing your mind.

Michael rose to his feet. "Let's go. I'm freezing." He grabbed my hand, helped me to my feet—and tugged me right to him.

Again, I could feel his warm breath on my lips.

I clung to the elbow of Michael's sleeve as his eyes tracked back and forth, searching mine. It took every ounce of willpower to keep myself from asking him what he was looking for.

Somewhere deep inside, I already knew.

Michael lowered his chin and adjusted the zipper on my jacket, dragging it up slow. His voice was breathless, soft—tentative. "I don't want you to get cold."

I managed a whispered, "Thanks," between thunderous heartbeats. The game we were playing was becoming too real. We needed to head back. "We should go …"

During the trek back, Michael's chattier self returned. By the time we'd reached his car, I knew his entire schedule for the next week, including the finer details of what he was planning for each of the songs being recorded. It was fascinating stuff, and I found myself being pulled into his world. Michael had the best job on the planet as far as I was concerned.

I slid into the passenger seat and removed my gloves, still thinking about the technical skill, musical intelligence, and gifted artistry required to do Michael's job.

Before I had a chance to launch into a new conversation, Michael reached for the stereo, B.B King filling the cab as we drove out of the park.

The dingy pub and pool hall in downtown Denver hadn't been on my roster of regular stops for many years. Not since I was barely legal to walk through its doors.

I'd laughed upon seeing the decrepit establishment and proceeded to share a few fond memories of my misspent youth in the place, so Michael had insisted we stop and check the place out.

"This will be fun." Michael slapped me on the back and gripped the back of my neck as we stepped inside and scanned the interior, looking for a spot to sit. We were both starving, and from what I could remember, the food hadn't been bad here …but that was a long time ago.

"I haven't played pool in forever."

Michael pulled a chair out from the wooden four-place table situated off to one side of the room. "Me either, but I'm sure we'll muddle through."

"I won't be laying down any bets, that's for sure."

Michael smirked. "You're no fun."

"I'm fun …just not stupid. You could be a shark."

"I wish." Michael hung his jacket on the back of his chair and took a seat.

I flipped over the solitary menu, scanning it for something with a few carbs. I hadn't eaten breakfast, and my stomach was angry. I'd been in a hurry to get to Denver.

Michael tapped his fingers on the table, then leaned back and crossed his arms. "So, did you ever come here with Rebecca?"

I laughed. "Not so much. It wasn't her scene."

"Oh, come on ..." Michael smiled at me, his eyes shimmering with amusement. "What's not to like? You've got everything you need here. Beer, food, billiards—and excellent company to hang with. It looks like they even have bands playing here on occasion."

Michael pointed toward a raised platform that acted as a stage at the far end of the room. The only thing on it, an old upright piano.

"And see that." Michael looked back at me, his eyes animated like a small child's who's been given a puppy. "That there. That is music in a box. That's what that is."

I shrugged. "Sure, if I knew how to play it."

"Ha, well." Michael rose to his feet. "That's where I come in."

No way.

Michael jumped onto the stage, tipped open the piano lid, and pulled the bench out. He took a seat and stretched out his hands. I could tell Michael was using the time to run through a Rolodex of song choices in his head. He had a habit of licking his lips when he was thinking.

When he set his long, lean fingers to the keys, ...and the first few notes spilled into the space, I felt an emotional tug nearly hauling me out of my seat toward him.

I had not seen that coming.

Not one bit.

Michael's ability to play or my body's response to him doing so.

I shifted in my seat and leaned back in my chair to listen. Relaxing, a wide grin crept across my face as Michael began playing his own rendition of Eddie Boyd's *Five Long Years*, then slid his voice in, low and soulful, accompanying his own inspired interpretation with the lyrics.

It was brilliant.

Michael was brilliant.

He was mesmerizing to watch, theatrical, and talented—an expert in the art of entertainment. A consummate professional who had obviously spent a lot of time on stage.

I couldn't take my eyes off him.

Occasionally, Michael would glance in my direction and smile at me, raising my heart rate significantly. I had to admit, in addition to being gifted, Michael had the looks to pull it off.

Sensual and accomplished.

Michael Sanderson was sex set to music.

But what did I know?

A round of applause followed as Michael wrapped up. His responding grin brightened every corner of the room. The cocky bow before he stepped off the stage had me laughing.

Michael had shone on that stage. He was at home there.

It suited him.

"So, what do you think?" Michael slipped into the chair adjacent to mine.

"I'm blown away, Michael. Seriously." I set my hand on his arm, exhilarated. "When did you pick that up? You never played when you were living in Longmont, did you?"

"No," Michael nodded his thanks to the bartender as the middle-aged, weary-looking server set two beer in front of us, presumably on the house, as we hadn't ordered anything.

It was only then I realized my hand was still on Michael's arm.

I snatched it back, hoping the server hadn't noticed.

Michael smiled at me, amusement sparkling in his eyes. "That was part of the deal I struck with my parents when we moved to New York. I wouldn't cause a fuss if they enrolled me in piano and guitar lessons."

My mouth must have dropped open because a smirking laugh rolled up from the depths of Michael's chest. "What?"

"You play guitar too?"

"Absolutely. I've done more stage work with my guitar than I have on the piano. But mostly, I use the skills I've picked up to act as a session musician when I'm working on a recording."

I shook my head in wonderment. "You're quite the catch, aren't you?"

Where the hell did that come from?

Michael's knee bumped against mine and stayed there. "You think so?"

He was watching me with subtle curiosity, his thick lashes obscuring my view of his eyes only briefly every few seconds.

I'm not sure how long I waited to answer that question.

I sucked a breath into my lungs. I hadn't realized I'd been holding it.

Sex set to music.

What is wrong with you, Ryan?

I looked down at my beer. "Yeah, sure." I hazarded a glance at Michael, but he had made a similar move, looking away and lifting a beer to his lips, withdrawing contact from my knee.

"I guess so," I rambled on. "I mean, when you're out there playing to audiences, you must have women clambering all over you."

"Sometimes." Michael tipped his head to one side and shrugged. "I generally avoid picking up women who have spent their entire evening drinking. I like to get to know someone before I sleep with them. And that generally isn't on the menu after a gig."

A huffing sound escaped my throat.

"I'll have to take your word on that one."

Michael scratched at his beard and made a one-hundred-and-eighty-degree turn in our conversation. "I'm toying with the idea of shaving this off."

God, no.

The urge to reach out and touch the bristly hair was strong. Just to rub the back of my knuckles across it. The memory of when he'd hugged me at my door, the abrasiveness of his beard against my bristly cheek, my heart skipped a beat, a crimson blush heating my face.

I cleared my throat and peered into my beer as if I might find the reason for my body's response to Michael somewhere in the bottom of the glass.

I shook my head. "I think you should keep it."

"Yeah? Why?" Michael's voice was low, whispering—almost seductive.

I looked up, my heart thundering—and wandered aimlessly into the emerald pools of his eyes—with no hope of finding my way out.

What I was feeling for Michael was much more than a need to be near him.

"Ryan ...," Michael whispered, reminding me he'd asked me a question.

I glanced down at Michael's lips, marveling at the contrast

of dark blond against pink, then followed the coarse hairs back to his eyes. "It looks good on you."

My answer seemed to satisfy Michael. He leaned back in his chair and flagged down our server, asking for a second menu.

After a few moments of perusing the food options on offer, Michael's leaned toward me. "So, what do you think? What looks good?"

My heart thumped heavy in my chest.

You.

You look good.

Tears pinched at the corners of my eyes as the words I toyed with saying formed in my mind.

It would be a joke, of course.

Of course.

"Ryan," Michael said softly. "Are you all right?"

The truth is, I had no idea if I was all right. Out of nowhere, Michael had developed an allure about him that had me sucking in shallow breaths. I hadn't a clue how I'd ended up here.

Guys weren't supposed to become this infatuated with their guy friends, that much I knew for sure. Maybe I was coming down with something. An impending flu would explain my light-headedness, and the fiery sensation buzzing through my body.

"I'm fine." I set the menu down. "I'm going to have a clubhouse sandwich.".

"Do you want another beer?"

I hadn't realized I'd drained the first one. My throat was unusually scratchy and dry. I was definitely coming down with something.

"Just one more," I replied after too much thought. "I can't have you beating me at pool."

"You needn't worry about that." Michael grinned. "Make

that two clubhouse sandwiches, and two more beer," he said to the server who'd appeared at our table.

I leaned back, crossed my arms, and looked around the room, trying to restore my thoughts to a place of normality. People were glancing in our direction, smiling, and whispering praise for Michael's performance, curious as to whether he was someone famous. Michael was an incredibly talented guy, and he was my friend—my best friend.

The concept gave me a ripple of shivers.

I was proud of him …proud to be with him.

Michael bumped me with his knee. "So, going back to our earlier conversation about women, have you started dating yet?"

"No." I shook my head. "Janice is always on me about it, but I'm not ready." I fixed my attention on Michael's eyes as I continued. I'm not sure why. "You? Any prospects?"

Michael rolled his eyes and stretched out his arms, reclining in his chair, and released a long, exasperated sigh. "My ex, Brenda and I went on a *date* last week."

"How did that go?"

"Terrible."

"I'm sorry." I did my best to circumnavigate the smile threatening to appear on my face by lifting my second beer to my lips. I took a sip and set the glass back on the table. *What the hell is wrong with you?* "It would be good for the kids if you got back together with her."

"Maybe," Michael replied, "but it's highly unlikely. Our getting back together. Or a reconciliation being beneficial for the kids. We're too far apart on so much stuff."

"Do you mind if I ask what happened?"

Michael sighed and ran his hand through his hair. Two bulky, silver rings on his fingers caught the light, his bicep and left pec flexing hard and smooth beneath his black t-shirt.

I couldn't imagine what would cause a woman to discard him. Michael was the most caring, honest, and sincere person I'd ever met. And that was saying something. My Rebecca had also held those qualities. It was one of the things I'd loved about her.

"Brenda was convinced I was cheating on her. She never understood the long hours required to produce a quality recording. She thought for sure I was seeing someone."

"So, she still doesn't believe you …?"

"I postponed our recent date at the last minute. It was scheduled for the day following the night I drove to your place. I was too tired to even contemplate going a few rounds with her."

Michael thanked the server as she set our plates in front of us. The sandwiches didn't look half-bad. I turned my plate so Michael could move the slices of dill pickle off his sandwich and onto mine. Pineapples and pickles. Two things I knew Michael absolutely hated.

And apparently, Michael hadn't forgotten how much I loved pickled anything.

"What did you tell her was the reason for canceling?"

"I told her it was none of her business. So, of course, she kept pushing. I eventually told her I was helping an old friend. That I stayed overnight and needed to catch up on some sleep."

Michael picked up one half of his sandwich, and held it, poised near his mouth. He smiled and winked at me. "I suppose I could've clarified that it was a guy friend. But it's an issue of trust. After all these years, she should know me well enough to know I would never cheat on her—"

Michael bit down on his sandwich, signifying the finality of his opinion on the matter. He was right, he could've explained. But then, why should Michael have to. Whether he was seeing someone or not was none of Brenda's business. They weren't together anymore.

Then why had Michael referred to his non-existent indiscretions as *cheating* on her?

"Michael. Even though you're divorced, are you still committed to Brenda?"

Michael smiled and brushed the crumbs off his fingers. "Why? Do you have plans to set me up with someone?"

I shrugged. "You never know. Someone may come along who's interested."

"Like who?" Michael licked some mayonnaise from his lips, sending my heart into a deafening and realistic rendition of cardiac arrest.

"I …um." *Goddamn it, Ryan. Pull it together*. "No one in particular."

"That's too bad. I'd like to find someone I could share my life with again. Except, this time, I'd like to find someone who understands me and what drives me. Someone who is great with my kids and shares my passion for music."

"Yeah, …um." I cleared my throat. "That would be great."

"But—" Michael slammed his hands down on the table and rose to his feet. "How am I supposed to meet a woman when I rarely leave my recording studio?" He jerked his thumb toward one of the pool tables. "Ready for a game?"

The rest of the afternoon was uneventful. We played a few rounds of pool, drove around Denver a bit more, and I listened to Michael regale me with stories of his teenage years growing up in Manhattan. His parents had done well for themselves, forming their own law firm within a few years of moving. Michael had led a somewhat charmed life after leaving Longmont. Expensive homes, clothes, …cars. All the trappings of the Upper East Side, which explained a lot.

I adjusted the passenger side seat belt. My chest had begun to feel tight as Michael talked about life with his ex-wife, Brenda. He had loved her once, but it had never been reciprocated.

He'd met her through his parents' firm where she'd started as a legal assistant. Oddly, the details of their meeting sounded forced, much like an arranged marriage.

"Are you sure Brenda never loved you?"

Michael tightened his grip on the steering wheel and turned into the parking lot at Inspiration Point, where I'd left my car. Where we'd begun our day. Where we'd stepped over more lines.

"She used to say it, but she never showed it. Her career came first." Michael turned to face me after switching off the engine. "We almost didn't have children. She couldn't see the point."

"What changed her mind?"

"I don't know." Michael shook his head. "My parents maybe. With me being their only child, they were anxious to have us gift them with grandchildren."

"Sounds a bit mechanical."

"No, it was fine. I wanted to have kids."

The thought of Michael and Brenda together in bed made me cringe. How could Michael have sex with someone so emotionally disconnected from him?

On that same topic, Michael had squirmed out of answering the question I'd asked him earlier in the pub. Whether he was still committed to Brenda even though they were divorced.

"Are you still having sex with her?" It was a bold personal question, but I felt as though Michael and I had reached a point in our relationship where we could talk about anything.

What had Michael meant about cheating on her?

Michael didn't seem to mind. No puzzled or indignant looks were fired my way. Only curiosity. A prickly, burning sensation crept up my neck to my cheeks.

"Why do you want to know?" Michael replied after deafening moments of silence. His question caught me off guard.

Why?

He was skirting around the question again.

"Because I want you to be happy. If continuing a *relationship* with Brenda is what does it for you, then I'm all for it." I shifted in my seat. Michael's eyebrows were raised; warm brown, questioning arches above seas of emerald green—as if he didn't believe me.

Michael leaned his head against the headrest, watching me—tracking every movement I made. His breathing ragged, his lashes standing on guard, his mouth still—his lips…

Dammit.

Bursts of air billowed in and out of my nostrils. Parting my lips to breathe would only serve to fuel my imagination. I leaned in closer to Michael, regardless.

His warm breath rolled past my chin.

Would it be such a bad thing? Kissing him. Just as friends. The night on the sofa with him, curled into his arms, holding my hand, comforting me. It had felt so damn good.

Michael licked his lips. "What if I told you I was still sleeping with her?"

I jerked away from him as if I'd been burned. "Are you?"

"No." Michael straightened up and rubbed a hand across his mouth, looking as stunned as I felt. Something had almost happened between us. I'm not sure what, but I suspected it wouldn't have ended with a simple kiss.

It was time for me to go.

I grabbed the door handle and opened the door. "I should get going."

"Sure, yeah."

"Okay …" I set my foot on the ground, prepared to remove myself from the car, but Michael reached out and grabbed my arm before I had a chance to leave.

I took a deep breath, tempering my response to his touch. If he intended to haul me back into that car, I knew I wouldn't be able to muster enough willpower to resist him.

"Ryan." Michael released my arm. "I don't have the kids again next weekend. Brenda and I switched weekends so I could have the kids with me over Thanksgiving."

I steadied my breathing.

I knew what Michael was asking me, or at least I thought I did.

"I'll have to check with Janice."

Our next meeting wouldn't be as friends. "Denver or Longmont?"

Either would do.

"Denver." Michael leaned back in his seat, watching me. "I have a band I want you to see."

My stomach dropped. Not what I was expecting him to say, but maybe I'd misunderstood. Perhaps I'd been too wrapped up in my own assumptions to interpret his intent correctly.

"I'll call you after I talk to Janice."

"Excellent."

"Okay, right, …see you."

"Ryan, wait." Michael's grabbed a hold of my hand. He stroked his thumb back and forth across it—shy and uneasy as if he had more to say.

More he wanted to do.

I hadn't been mistaken about Michael's intentions.

The urge to climb back into that car with him, haul him into the backseat, attack his mouth—and explore every inch of him was strong.

Michael exhaled as he looked at me and released my hand. "Drive safe."

I slipped into my car, my carefully cultivated beliefs about myself destroyed. Michael had blown my world wide open. In a few short days, he had taken me from zero to I want to rip his clothes off. The flu theory wasn't holding water. I hadn't felt this healthy in years.

I pulled onto the highway, the drive home seeming longer than usual. Every mile taking me further and further away from where I wanted to be.

Chapter Six

"This is incredible!" I drummed my hand on the table in time to the music. Low bass, high snare— The blues band Michael had chosen for us to see was beyond all expectations. He'd somehow found a cover ensemble that captured the LP collection of my youth.

I was in reminiscence heaven.

"I heard these guys playing a couple of weeks ago," Michael shouted over the music and din of the crowd seated around us. "I made a note to keep track of where they were playing."

"They're fantastic."

"My way of saying thank you." Michael clapped an arm around my shoulders, pulling me closer, sending a trickle of warmth down my spine. I breathed up into the sensation, encouraging it to spread around me like an embrace.

"For introducing me to the music of my soul," he added.

I nearly choked on my beer. Michael's attempt to keep a straight face after that dramatic statement had me gulping hard to keep the amber liquid from reaching my lungs.

Michael's pursed lips popped open, tears streaming down his face, and he broke into a goofy grin that erupted into rolling, raucous laughter—exuding absolute, abundant, authentic joy.

"You're an ass." I nudged Michael, causing him to release me.

I leaned back in my chair and looked over at him, still smiling and chuckling to himself as he watched the band. It made me smile.

Michael's contentment was contagious, his charm— seductive.

I cleared my throat and returned to enjoying the band. There hadn't been a single moment of tension between Michael and me since I'd arrived at the bar three hours ago.

No mention of the intimacy on the walk …or in Michael's car afterward.

Just a couple of friends hanging out for the night. A few drinks. A few dances with the steady stream of women Michael was attracting. Everything was good …great even.

Perhaps it was better if we kept it that way.

I tapped Michael's arm with my hand and leaned toward him. "Are you sure it's all right for me to crash at your place? I could always cab it home."

"All the way to Longmont. Don't be ridiculous." Michael's expression shifted, contemplation forming creases around his eyes. "Is everything all right?"

"Yeah, I'm fine." The music trailed off, signaling the end of the second set. I shifted in my seat and lifted my pint glass from the table. I was surprised by the absence of beer, even though I'd noted earlier that it was empty. "Maybe a bit too much to drink."

I motioned toward the door. "Do you want to get out of here and grab some food before we head back to your place?"

Michael rose to his feet. "Lead the way."

I stared at the gleaming, black-and-chrome Harley Davidson angle-parked in front of the bar as Michael handed me a helmet. I glanced at his attire. The jeans, leather jacket, and motorcycle boots he was wearing should have given it away. The guy was full of surprises.

The plan had been to leave my car behind at the bar if I drank too much—an inevitability after the week I'd had. However, I hadn't known Michael owned a motorcycle, or that I'd be expected to climb on it with him, especially this close to the end of November.

Michael smirked at me as he slipped on his gloves. "What?"

I stepped toward the bike, running my hand along its lustrous, black leather seat. "Who are you? And what have you done with my baby brother's geeky friend?"

"Yeah, I've changed a bit since then."

"No, kidding." I zipped the front of my coat up. "We're going to freeze to death."

Michael's soft laughter was dampened as he lowered the visor on his helmet. "There's a diner less than seven blocks from here. You'll be fine." He swung his leg over the bike, flicked back the kickstand, and balanced the motorized, metal beast. "Get on."

"I'm drunk. What if I fall off?"

A snort of amusement from Michael made me grin. I wasn't that drunk. I was stalling, and he knew it. My reason for stalling— disconcerting, but the thought of having my chest plastered against Michael's back, my hands clinging to him—was churning up my gut.

Maybe I wasn't ready for this.

Whatever *this* was.

I pulled the helmet onto my head.

Get on.

Gripping both of Michael's shoulders, I hoisted myself onto the seat behind him and settled my hands on his waist. The rush of longing was immediate. I found myself suspended precariously in a bizarre reality chasm, stranded somewhere between wanting to press my body closer to Michael's and feeling as if I might break down in tears.

This was so far beyond my comfort zone.

I was second-guessing pretty much everything.

I closed my eyes and allowed my chest to press up against Michael's broad, muscular back. He felt good. This man bore no resemblance to the little kid I'd known.

Michael's body shook with laughter as he started up the bike. The words, "don't crush my ribcage," were barely audible above the noise of the engine.

A few revs, and we were on our way, peeling off down the street. After the first couple of smooth turns, I relaxed, loosening my grip.

Much sooner than I anticipated, Michael pulled into the parking lot of an all-night diner. I reluctantly shifted my hands onto the edge of the seat as he shut off the motor and set the kickstand.

He removed his helmet and looked at me over his shoulder.

"Are we stopping for food?" Michael asked quietly, his intense green eyes tracking back and forth, attempting to detect any trace of my expression behind the tinted visor of my helmet.

The muscles of my stomach quivered in response.

There was something new in the way Michael was watching me. I took an inventory, not wanting to speculate on what might be happening. Michael's breath was hesitant—nervous almost as it buffeted steadily against the visor between us.

"Ryan?" Michael lowered his hand to rest on my thigh, squeezing it, fracturing all illusions of my misreading the situation. It was only then I realized I was gripping Michael's leather jacket, clutching him to me as if he were my very own life preserver.

I wanted so much more from this man than friendship.

I whispered, "No," beneath my breath and shook my head.

Michael nodded, pulled the helmet back onto his head, and fired up the bike. The remaining distance to Michael's apartment whirred by, my vision unfocused, my mind in a loop. It was possible, still, that there had been a miscommunication, and Michael simply thought I was tired. That my objection to stopping for food had nothing to do with the feel of his warm hand on my thigh. Perhaps he'd sensed it …perhaps he hadn't, but there was no denying—the thought of his hand traveling further up my leg had my body buzzing.

I'm sorry, Rebecca, I can't stop this…

I wanted to feel Michael's hands on my bare skin.

The realization nearly brought me to tears. It was one thing wanting to be closer to Michael; it was another thing entirely wanting to be naked with him.

Michael leaned back slightly, prompting me to decide. It took a full two blocks, but eventually, driven by the need to know if I'd imagined Michael's intent, I embraced him, placing one hand on his stomach and allowing the other to wander up along the zipper of his jacket to his chest. I fanned my gloved fingers out, gripped his pec, and clung to him.

The vibration created by his hum of approval reached my chest.

It was at that point, my cock stirred.

I nearly let go of Michael entirely.

"Are you all right back there?" Michael shouted as he pulled into the underground parking of his building and shut off his bike.

"Fine. Yeah, …fine." Panic fluttered in my chest. I hadn't thought this through. I was letting a guy take me back to his place.

A guy.

No, not just any guy.

Michael.

I gripped onto Michaels's shoulders as he parked his bike and set the kickstand. My hand ran down his arm to steady myself as he dismounted. He removed his helmet and brushed his gloved hand across his hair, smoothing it back into place.

I just sat there.

I was terrified to get off the bike. Terrified to find out if the feelings I was having were real. Terrified to find out if Michael was truly feeling those same urges.

"Ryan." Michael unlatched the strap on my helmet, lifted it from my head, and brushed his fingers through my hair. "I can't let you stay out here."

I nodded. "Yeah, …cold."

Michael flashed me one of his disarming smiles. "Something like that."

Walking into Michael's apartment, the magnitude of the space caught me off guard.

"Wow, you're doing well," I stammered like an idiot. The modern, sleek elegance of the place wasn't what I had been expecting. Although I should have. Michael's clothes were always designer, his family vehicle a Mercedes SUV. And his bike …his motorbike was gorgeous.

Michael began stripping off his gloves and leather jacket in the front entry as I stood there, gawking. Every movement of his body captivated me.

Like a damned, drooling teenager, I couldn't take my eyes off him.

Apparently, the bike wasn't the only thing I found gorgeous.

My attention wandered from Michael's broad shoulders to the cut of his jeans as he hung up his jacket.

My breath shuddered in my chest. Every bit of him enticed me.

Michael rolled up his sleeves as he walked toward me, his muscled forearms accentuating his pure maleness. "Can I get you another drink, or do you want a glass of water instead?"

"Water, please," I stammered, then wandered off in the direction of the floor-to-ceiling window in the living room. Denver stretched out below us, yawning toward the horizon.

Mesmerized by the view, I jumped when Michael's hand touched my arm.

"Sorry," he said.

"No, it's all right." I accepted the tall, crystal glass filled halfway with ice water, but found I wasn't as thirsty as I thought.

"Are you sure you're all right?" Michael set his hand on the small of my back.

"Not really, no." A part of me wanted to run, but a more compelling piece of me wanted to stay and see this through. It was Michael. My best friend. And right now, I wanted to know him in ways I never would have entertained when we'd run into each other in that coffee shop.

"The night I drove out to your place ...," Michael whispered in my ear. He was standing behind me, so incredibly close, I could feel his breath on the back of my neck. I trembled as he reached around and removed the glass from my hand and set it on a nearby side table.

"I know." My voice couldn't have been quieter. "Something shifted."

Michael set his hands on my hips. "I haven't been able to stop thinking about how you felt in my arms."

I sighed. Once again, almost brought to tears. I couldn't stop this. My feelings for this man who'd reappeared in my life so unexpectedly—unstoppable.

I leaned back into his embrace.

God, he feels good.

Michael wrapped his arms around me and kissed the back of my neck, sending apprehensive shocks of pure lightening rocketing down my spine.

I swallowed hard, my mind screaming at me to stop.

I couldn't do this.

"I'm sorry. I can't …" I pulled away and turned to face Michael. He looked as unsure as I felt. His brow was drawn, creased with concern—his breath rapid.

I wanted to go to him, calm his fears.

I took a step toward him, intending to crack a joke to break the tension. Bring us back to the point in our relationship where things had been simpler. Where we'd been just friends.

I couldn't do it.

My hand found its way to Michael's face. I cupped his cheek and brushed my thumb across the bristles of his beard. A strange sensation in someone I was craving so fiercely.

Our hesitant breath mingled for a moment before I gave into my desire.

I descended on Michael's mouth, slow and tender, testing my response to kissing him. My chest swelled, my heart stricken with the pureness of the moment. Michael's hands traveled down my back to my ass, drawing me closer to him, his lips so soft and receptive beneath mine.

Far too receptive.

The pureness turned carnal, my mouth taking control of his. I propelled Michael across the room, and secured him against the far wall, surprising even myself. Michael was churning up an aggressive hunger in me I hadn't known I'd been harboring.

Groaning with reciprocated need, Michael's hands were busy loosening my shirt, hauling it out from where it had been tucked into my jeans. My hands were on him; everywhere I could grab hold of him. His shoulders, his back …his ass. His mouth enthralling me as we dove deeper.

The tug and clink of my belt being wrenched open startled me. I placed my hand on Michael's chest, pushing him away, and took a few steps back.

What the hell am I doing?

I stood there, fixed in place, unable to retreat any further. I knew exactly what I was doing.

The panic subsided.

I wanted him, and he knew it.

Michael closed the gap between us and finished unbuckling my belt, his lips pressed against mine, biting and sucking them into his mouth. I was helpless to object.

Oh, Christ.

I nearly melted into Michael as he undid the button and fly of my pants and pushed his hand in past the waistband of my boxers. The feel of his cool hand on my cock, gripping—stroking, sent my mind reeling. Everything I thought I knew about my sexuality spiraled out of existence.

The taste of Michael's lips, his beard against mine, the deep sounds rolling up from his chest, …and the steady pull of his hand—longing and desperation filled me.

I pressed Michael against the wall, causing him to groan seductively.

The sound of him. The scent of him.

So alive—so male.

It undid me.

Each pulse ripped through me, thrusting me hard against him, wetting us both in my warmth as Michael's lips remained nuzzled against my ear, whispering words of affection.

How much I meant to him.

How much he'd wanted me.

It was too much. A flush of embarrassment rose in my cheeks, and I pulled away, awkwardly fumbling with my pants to set them right, the inside of my boxers, sticky and wet against my stomach. The flush in my face turned into more of a stinging burn.

What have I done?

I made my way over to the sofa when Michael headed for what I assumed was the washroom. I could hear him in there washing his hands.

When Michael came back into the room, he just stood there silently, looking at me. He peered over at a doorway off the living room, then back at me.

"Are you coming to bed with me? Or do you want to stay on the sofa?" He'd obviously picked up on my discomfort about what had transpired between us.

I swallowed hard and sat down. "I think I should stay out here."

The level of hurt my rejection caused was obvious, but Michael simply nodded. "There are blankets and pillows in the hall closet."

Standing in his doorway, Michael studied me for a moment. "I don't suppose you'll be here in the morning."

I didn't reply, but my silence was answer enough. Michael pressed his bedroom door closed with a click.

I only lasted about four hours. Enough time to sober up so I could drive.

I called a cab to take me back to my car.

The icy condition of the roads aside, my drive home was fraught with uncertainty. Despite rejecting that caring, exuberant, gorgeous man, I longed to be near him. To be curled up in Michael's bed, his arms holding me—his lips kissing the back of my neck.

It made no sense.

Everything I was feeling made no sense.

This wasn't who I was.

Chapter Seven

The mayhem of a Middleton Thanksgiving dinner would have typically made me smile. The family room was lit up with premature Christmas tree lights, music, and the laughter of family.

Sam had found his way down the mountain to be with us this year, intending to stay until Christmas. He'd taken up residence in my guest room for the night, promising to move to my parents' house in the morning. A relocation that eased my discomfort somewhat.

Despite the fact Sam was my brother, it felt as though he was intruding. The room he was staying in, the one directly across the hall from my own, had been Michael's when he'd stayed overnight with his kids. Having my brother in it reminded me how much I wished it was occupied by someone else. It had taken a great deal of effort to erase the memory of Michael's voice radiating up from the kitchen as he prepared breakfast.

Who was I kidding? It still haunted me. We hadn't spoken since that night—the night when we'd obliterated the line—and destroyed our friendship.

"Are you all right?" Janice asked me, placing a hand on my shoulder. "You've been in a funk all week."

"Tired, that's all."

"Are you sure? You can talk to me, you know."

"I know, but I'm fine." I turned around and offered her a weak smile. "Honestly."

"I don't believe you."

"That's your prerogative." I reached for the oven mitts and opened the oven door. The turkey only had another thirty minutes according to the timer, but I wanted to check its temperature. One of the things Rebecca had passed on to me before she died was how to plan and implement a large family dinner with turkey and all the fixings. She would've been proud of me.

This Thanksgiving was supposed to have been different. I'd been all geared up for Michael to help me with dinner, imagining all sorts of scenarios where we'd end up in each other's arms again—his lips meeting mine for the first time—sweet and soft.

That was behind me now.

The image destroyed—sullied by what we'd done.

"Talk to me."

"Drop it, Janice. I'm fine."

"Ryan—"

My phone rang from where I'd set it on the counter. I closed the oven door and threw my gloves onto the counter. The call display lit up with the name *Mikey*. I chose to ignore it. I'd even considered removing Michael's number from my phone completely.

Our relationship was ruined.

There was no point dragging the inevitable out any longer.

"Aren't you going to answer that?" Janice asked, attempting to hand me my phone. "Ryan, come on, it's Michael." She crossed her arms, still holding my phone. It stopped ringing. "Did you two have an argument or something? Is that why you're in such a bad mood?"

The phone started ringing again.

"Something like that, yeah."

"You should talk to him."

"I don't want to talk to him."

"Don't be such an ass." Janice shoved the phone into my hand. "Talk to him."

I exhaled an exasperated sigh and gave in to my sister's insistence, accepting the call.

"Hey."

"Ryan," was all Michael said in response, his voice rough, deep, and pure. Hearing him say my name was enough to send my heart racing, bringing back a range of emotions I'd been working to subdue. There was no place in my life for where our friendship had taken us.

"Why are you calling?"

Janice nudged me, a look of concern painting her face.

"I called to say Happy Thanksgiving." A long pause followed, only interrupted intermittingly by his hesitant breath. "Ryan, I think we need to talk about what happened."

"I have nothing to say." I wandered off toward the back hall, away from my sister's prying ears. "It was a mistake, Michael. What happened between us was a mistake."

"How can you say that? It didn't feel like a mistake until you decided to blow me off. You shouldn't have left without talking to me first. If you had come to bed, instead of sleeping on that damned sofa, we could've talked it through."

"Michael, drop it."

"Ryan …"

"Stop. I'm not interested, all right?"

"Fine. If that's the way you want to play this." Michael's voice had turned cold, distant. "But I don't see why we have to blow up our friendship over it."

"We can't go back to the way things were, Michael."

"We don't have to. Surely, we can move forward from this."

"I don't think we can."

"Ryan, please. I miss you." The softness in his voice had returned, crushing my heart. Perhaps I'd been too hasty. Maybe we could talk this through.

"I know, I—"

Sam raced down the hall and slid up beside me, leaping with excitement. "Janice says you have Mikey on the phone. Hand it over."

Before I had a chance to react, Sam snatched the phone from my hands and launched into an animated conversation with Michael.

I'd been about to tell Michael I missed him too.

Having that opportunity stolen from me was probably a good thing. Listening to the achingly familiar sound of Michael's voice any longer would've sucked me back in.

Which was the last thing I needed.

I still fell asleep each night craving his touch.

The longing often brought me to tears.

Much as it was doing now.

"I'm surprised Michael changed his mind about Thanksgiving dinner." My mom had snuck up behind me in the kitchen, startling me. "Sam would have loved to have seen him."

I took a covert swipe at the tears gathering in the corners of my eyes and turned to face her. "He ended up with other family commitments at the last minute, Mom."

"That's too bad, but not surprising. It *is* the start of the holiday season, after all."

"That it is."

The sound of Cindy shrieking with delight, at something my dad had told her, pulled my mind away from obsessing over Michael.

Taylor, Cindy, and Marcus. They were my focus.

Somehow, I'd lost sight of that.

I followed my mom into the family room and immersed myself in the joys of family. We were all together this holiday season, and that was a rare thing—an incredibly precious thing.

Yet somehow, even with my family gathered around me, it was apparent something—someone was missing in my life. I couldn't shake the anguish running rampant in my heart.

Two weeks passed before I heard from Michael. Enough time without seeing him for me to work through what had happened in his apartment that night.

I'd known he'd call again eventually.

It wasn't over between us.

I sat down on one of the benches situated strategically around the playground in the local park. Marcus was on a play date, and we'd opted to head outdoors. The two ruffians had been tearing around in the house at speeds that threatened to destroy the place.

I accepted the call lighting up my phone. "Hey, Michael, how are you doing?"

"Better. I wasn't sure you'd take my call."

"I just needed some time."

"I figured." The sound of music in the background lessened in volume. Michael must've closed a door to gain some privacy. "I'm sorry if I pushed you into something you didn't want to do, Ryan."

"You didn't. I was a willing participant." I moved the phone to my other ear. "Let's place it in the archive of failed experiments and leave it at that, okay?"

"Done."

"So, where do we go from here?"

"Well, I have my niece's wedding to go to in Longmont this weekend. It's early in the day, with no reception worth mentioning."

"A December wedding. Brave."

"More like crazy." A short pause. "I was hoping to see you. It doesn't have to be much. I could come by the house, hang with you and the kids for a while. If that's all right."

I smiled. Michael was obviously having the same concerns as me. That interacting might be awkward between us initially. Having the kids there provided us with something to focus on.

"That works for me. What time?"

"Saturday, around four. I won't have the kids with me."

"Cindy and Marcus will survive. They still talk about the crafting extravaganza we put together for them. They had a blast. Even Taylor."

Michael laughed, warming me through. "One of our more insane ideas."

"*One* of them, yeah." I ran a hand through my hair, rose to my feet, and started pacing around the outer circle of the playground, keeping a sharp eye on Marcus and his friend.

"No more mention of that, remember?"

"Right, sorry." I laughed, glad we were in full agreement about moving beyond that awkward subject without delving into the why's and how's.

"I'd love to keep talking, but I need to get back to work. We can catch up this weekend."

"Sure, yeah. We'll talk later." I sat back down, a rush of regret filling my chest. I could've easily spent the next few hours on the phone with Michael. I'd been missing our near-nightly phone calls; recalling our days and sharing stories of crazy events in our lives.

Soon.

I stuffed my phone in my coat pocket and reclined against the back of the bench seating, breathing easier. It was a beautiful day. Crisp but sunny, the kids were playing happily, and I was going to be seeing Michael again soon.

A winter day couldn't possibly get much better than that.

The chimes of the doorbell rang through the house, their tinny calls drifting into the backyard to where the kids and I had retreated. I placed my hand against the mesh of the trampoline's safety netting where my eldest was taking his turn leaping around, while the other two attempted to construct a snowman from the dusting of snow we'd received last night.

"Taylor, keep an eye on things for two seconds. I need to get the door."

His bouncing came to a standstill. "Sure thing, Dad."

"Thank you."

Slowly …very slowly, Taylor was beginning to step up when it came to watching his two younger siblings. He was still years away from being able to babysit, but that day would likely come before I was ready for it. He was growing up fast.

Slipping my winter boots off and nearly impaling my socked foot on a pile of Lego in the family room in my haste, I managed to arrive safely at the front door.

What awaited me as I swung the door open nearly brought me to my knees.

Michael, standing nervously on the front step, his lips parted, pink and full amidst a sea of neatly groomed hair, killing it in an expensive three-piece suit, cut to perfection; his crisp, white shirt deliberately unbuttoned at his throat, exposing an enticing sliver of bare skin.

"Hey." His full, thick lashes danced seductively, accentuating the depth of intensity to which he was watching me. When he smiled at me, the pull was stronger than I had any hope of resisting.

I reached forward, gripped the front of his suit jacket, and hauled him into the house.

It was like coming home.

Michael maneuvered me toward the wall, attacking my mouth with the hunger of a man who'd been starved to the point of delirium. My back slammed against the hard surface, rattling the light fixture. I gasped in response to his assault, the feel of being overpowered fueling me.

Michael's hands found their way up under my shirt, skimming their way up my back, clawing and grappling at my flesh, his hips grinding against mine, thrusting—dismantling my inhibitions.

I surrendered to him, mewling with desperation as he bit and sucked at the skin running from my jaw straight down to my shoulder, my arms encircling him, clenching handfuls of his ass through the fabric of his tailored suit—forcing him harder against me.

"God, I've missed you," I whispered, not sure how I'd managed to formulate any words at all. I placed a hand on his chest, my senses returning—marginally. "The kids."

Michael took a step back. "Right. I forgot about them."

"A hello like that will do that to a person."

I adjusted myself. My cock had swollen to visibly uncomfortable proportions. Not something I thought would be my reaction to reconnecting with any guy in my lifetime—ever.

"I have to be honest with you, Ryan." Michael followed me into the family room, where I had a clear view of the kids in the backyard through the sliding glass door. "I had every intention of coming over here, wiping the slate clean, and starting fresh with you …as friends." He jerked a thumb toward the front entry. "I had no idea *that* was going to happen."

"I think it surprised us both." Satisfied the kids were safely occupied, I reached for Michael and pulled him to me, landing a soft kiss on his lips. "I need to make a phone call."

Michael wrinkled his brow but didn't question me. I think he knew where I was going with this. Having my kids in the house wasn't something either of us wanted right now.

As soon as I'd seen Michael, my reluctance to accept what I felt for him had evaporated like sizzling water on a hot grill. I was drawn to this man in ways I'd never experienced before.

"Hey, Janice, can I ask you for a favor?"

"That depends. Does it involve doing any more of your laundry?"

"No." I peered over at Michael and smiled. "But, thank you for handling that for me."

Michael wandered up behind me and ran his hand down the center of my back to my ass, then set his teeth to my shoulder, biting me lightly. My cock responded, pressing against my zipper, clouding my ability to think clearly. We still had a few things to do before we could be alone.

"Janice, could the kids stay with you tonight?"

"Sure. What's up?"

"Nothing."

I glanced out the window. The kids were occupied with chasing each other around the yard. They hadn't noticed Michael was in the house.

I sucked in a breath as Michael's hand had found its way to my thigh, riding it with increasing pressure down to above my knee and back up to the crease of my groin. His thumb brushed across my cock, and the memory of his clenched hand stroking my bare flesh flooded in.

I swallowed hard. "Everything is fine. I just need a night to myself."

"Okay, I'm on my way out anyway. I can be there in thirty minutes or so."

Thirty minutes?

There was no way I could hold out that long. The possibility of me hauling Michael into the nearest washroom while the kids were still in the house was dangerously feasible.

"Is there any way you could pick them up first?" I grabbed Michael's hand to keep him from perusing further. I still needed to pass the kids off to my sister. An obvious boner wasn't something I wanted to greet her with when she arrived. "I've got a killer headache. I'd really appreciate it."

Janice sighed. "Sure, okay. Not my favorite thing though, big brother, taking them to the grocery store with me, but I can be there in five minutes."

"Thank you. You're a lifesaver."

I ended the call and turned to face Michael. The gorgeous green of his eyes, mere rings. I'd done that to him; our desire for one another undeniable.

I stepped in close and brushed my hand down the front of Michael's slacks. Biting my bottom lip, I was met with a throaty groan and a long, thick, rock-hard rod.

Fuck, I wanted him. The terror I had felt the first time I'd been overcome by these feelings wasn't there this time. A shiver ran through my belly, resulting in an ache in my balls.

My sister needed to get here fast.

"Where did you park your car?" There were semantics to be

dealt with. I didn't want my sister to know Michael was the reason I wanted the house to myself.

"On the street. I didn't want to block you in."

"Okay, good. Janice will start asking questions if she sees a car in the driveway." I headed for the stairs. "I need to gather up some overnight stuff for the kids."

"Let me do that." Michael touched my arm and started for the stairs. "Someone needs to keep an eye on the kids and get them ready. They don't know I'm here, and I think we should keep it that way if you don't want them blabbing about Uncle Mike being in the house."

"I'm sorry about that. I just don't want—"

"What's to be sorry about? I get it."

I watched Michael move up the stairs, the muscles of his ass being of particular interest. I groaned under my breath. My response to him was making my mind reel. Here was a guy—a guy who had been my little brother's best friend; a lanky, irritating kid with questionable hygiene. Now I was lusting after him with startling ferocity, our shared past, and his gender losing all relevance.

"Make sure you grab their toothbrushes and—"

"Ryan, stop." Michael grinned at me. "I know how to pack kids up for an overnight trip."

I smirked. "Sorry, I forgot."

"There will be more of that to come." Michael winked at me. "I have every intention of making you forget everything you've ever known."

"I'm going to hold you to that."

Michael's laughter filled the hall as he made his way to the kids' rooms. I smiled, my heart feeling lighter than it had in years. Michael, with his cheeky attitude, his warm and caring personality—his animated style of speaking, his expressive eyes, and his ability to make you feel as though you were the most important person in the world when he was with you.

He was everything I needed right now.

The knock at the door behind me startled me. I hadn't even organized the kids yet. I took off toward the backyard, shouting, "It's open," in my wake. I didn't want to waste time with pleasantries. Janice usually let herself in without any intervention on my part anyway.

"Are the kids ready?"

"Almost." I slid the glass door open. "Kids, Auntie Janice is here. She's taking you to her place for a sleepover."

Taylor crossed his arms. "I thought you said Uncle Mike was coming over today."

"Oh, um …" I ushered the other two in through the door. "He couldn't make it." Taylor didn't look convinced. "The wedding ran long."

"Yeah, right."

"Taylor, I have no control over that."

"I don't believe you." Taylor shuffled his way into the front hall behind me. "You probably said something to piss him off again."

"Taylor." Janice hauled Taylor into line with Cindy and Marcus. "Language."

She took the bags I handed her. The three knapsacks had made a covert appearance halfway down the stairs while Janice and I had been rounding up the kids in the family room.

"So, are you and Michael talking again?" Janice asked.

"In a manner of speaking, yeah."

Janice's eyes narrowed in contemplation, but she appeared to dismiss whatever was going through her mind. "I'm glad.

You've been a pain in everyone's ass since you stopped hanging out with him." She glanced up toward the top of the stairs. She suspected something. I wasn't showing any signs of having a headache. And I was obviously anxious for her to leave.

"Right," she said. "I'll leave you to it."

Hugs, kisses, and multiple good-byes, and the door finally closed behind them.

I looked up toward the upper landing. Michael was leaning against the wall, suit jacket discarded, dress shirt unbuttoned down to his waist. His expression—anxious but hungry.

I took the stairs two at a time.

Chapter Eight

The sound of the bedroom door clicking closed behind me brought on a multitude of overwhelming emotions. I looked past Michael to the king-sized mahogany bed. The last person to have shared the overstuffed bedding with me was my wife.

Instinctively, I touched the cool metal of my wedding band. Something I did every time I thought of my Rebecca.

Michael sensed my hesitation. "We can take this to the guest bedroom if you'd like."

I brought my attention back to him. Michael's eyes conveyed a deep concern for me. Even with the limited time we'd spent together, we'd become intimately connected.

I felt safe with him.

"No, I want to be here with you."

Michael touched my face. "You're sure this time. I don't want you to run out on me like that again." He released my face. "You hurt me, Ryan."

"I know. I'm sorry." I wrapped my arm around Michael's waist, drawing him to me. "Never again. I promise." I crushed my lips to his, slow and steady, biting—tasting, taking my time. The exchange was easy between us. As if we'd been on this journey with each other before.

I adjusted my grip and slipped my tongue past Michael's lips—immersing myself. A slow dance of our own making followed, the intensity of which almost brought me to tears.

Michael groaned against my lips, and his hands sprang to

life, gracefully completing the process of removing his shirt. He tossed it toward the chair in the corner of the room as I swayed against him, maneuvering him closer to the bed.

His hands slipped to my hips to guide me.

As the back of Michael's thighs touched the mattress, our lips parted. The furious pace of our previous encounter long forgotten. I brushed my fingers along Michael's collarbone, trying to memorize every detail. He sighed beneath my touch, submitting to me.

I slid my hand down his chest, raking my fingers through the dense, reddish hair, and around to the small of his back. Michael's skin was captivating. So taut against his lean muscle.

"I don't do well when you're not in my life, Michael."

"Me, either ..." Michael cradled my face in his hand and sought my lips—gentle and lazy; the kiss euphoric in its honesty. His arm wrapped around my waist and pulled me closer.

I had nothing to compare to how I felt for Michael as he devoured me. Overwhelming reverence, admiration—unity.

Maybe something more.

Michael sat down on the edge of the bed as I stripped my shirt off over my head. I pushed him back into the bedding and placed a single kiss in the middle of his chest, testing my commitment to taking this further.

Michael shifted, breathing up into the kiss and dug his fingers into my hair.

That was all the clarification I needed.

I wanted this.

With this man, I wanted this.

I brushed my lips across the hair on Michael's chest, inhaling the scent of soap, cologne, and perspiration; a combination I sensed over time would become an addiction.

Lowering my body onto his, I pursued the allure of Michael's skin, beginning at the base of his throat, nipping—licking, intoxicated by the primal maleness of him.

Michael's hands raked into my hair, attempting to drag me back to his mouth.

I wouldn't be persuaded—not yet. Michael quivered beneath me, mewling softly as I continued to satisfy my curiosity, tasting and teasing the tantalizing patch of skin shielding his pulse. His hips rolled up, the length of his hard cock briefly crushing against my own.

"Take your pants off," Michael whispered as his hands tugged at the waistband of my jeans.

I steadied a kiss on Michael's lips before taking his direction.

As I stood at the end of the bed and unfastened my jeans, I took a moment to study Michael lying there looking up at me,—waiting for me to return to him.

Watching him, my emotions plucked at my heart, hesitant as fingers on a harp ignited in flames.

Michael arched his back, lifting his ass from the bedding as I reached down and removed his dress slacks. They joined his shirt on the chair.

I could see the nervousness in Michael's eyes as I hooked my fingers into the waistband of his colorful briefs. They were failing miserably at hiding his arousal. Straining and damp, I guided them off his body, leaving him, and the effect I'd had on him, exposed.

Beautiful was the first word that came to my mind. Every contour of Michael's body toned; lustrous hair covering his chest and legs, growing denser around the base of his cock.

I caressed the heel of my hand down the front of my jeans.

It shocked me, my temptation. My mouth was watering at

the sight of him, his cock lying stiff, angled off to one side near his hip. Flushed pink, a beautiful arching bend extending along the entire length. I knew it would be smooth, velvety—aching for me to touch it.

Michael raised his arms and tucked his hands behind his head, setting off an unexpected surge of arousal. The hair beneath his arms offering me an entirely new territory warranting exploration.

I removed his socks and dropped them to the floor.

"Take them off," Michael whispered as he brought his arms back down and scooted up the distance of the bed. He adjusted a couple of pillows to support his head. I discarded my jeans and boxers, reducing them to a crumpled pile on the floor.

Michael's eyes visibly lit up.

When he licked his lips, my body reacted, my cock bobbing tight and hot in the cool air of the room. I crawled up between his legs, anxious to reach the security of his lips.

I needed my best friend to help soothe my nerves.

I took Michael's mouth, submerging myself in it, seeking the calm he always provided me. I was met with a level of blistering desire that wiped out any concerns I had about not knowing what we were supposed to be doing.

I had no doubt we'd figure it out together.

When our bodies made contact, skin against skin, our instincts took over. Michael undulated beneath me, rocking his hips as he locked onto my lips, grinding his cock against mine.

It was pure animalistic bliss. I matched his fervor, pinning him to the bed, thrusting, grunting—wanting more of him. Needing so much more.

I rose up on my hands and used my knees to encourage Michael to allow me more space between his legs. I angled my hips and stroked my cock along the length of Michael's, tantalizing in its subtlety—excruciatingly so.

Michael gasped, open-mouthed, and tipped his head back, digging his fingers into my arms. He looked every bit as gorgeous as a woman.

More so.

Michael's hands found their way onto my ass, encouraging me to take him to that place again. I dragged my cock along his, slow and deliberate—all the way to the base.

He smiled up at me. "Stop torturing me, would you."

"Not just you." I grinned at Michael. Every instant of pressure, every breathy response escalated my desire for him. I shifted his legs further apart. I wanted every damn bit of him.

Slow down.

Too soon...

Too fast...

I dropped to my elbows, reducing the space between us, our cocks becoming encased between the soft flesh of our bellies. The friction was incredible. Michael's gasping sighs transformed into throaty groans, his hips undulating up to meet mine with each thrust.

"Ryan ..." Michael whispered as he writhed beneath me. He arched his back, his shoulders nearly coming off the bed as he tipped his head back. Dragging his fingers up into my hair, he rolled his head to one side, directing me back toward his throat.

My mouth found its way back to the thrumming rhythm of his heartbeat. Teeth—lips, teasing and taunting his skin, the bristly hairs of his beard caressing my cheek. Michael groaned and rolled his hips up to meet me, his chest rising, filling.

"I'm going to cum," he whispered in my ear as he clawed at my back and wrapped his legs around mine, locking us together.

His feet were cold against my calves, the dense hair of his legs grazing against mine. It was an unusual sensation, a reminder of who was sharing my bed.

The thought slipped from my mind. I had a bond with Michael far beyond the physical attributes of his gender.

I pulled back so I could see Michael's eyes.

"Look at me."

My heart stammered as Michael opened his eyes for me. I hadn't thought it possible for the green coloring of them to become more intense. They drew me in. Glistening, emerald pools of pure sex. I was incapable of looking away.

"Ryan, I ..." Michael exhaled as he clung to me, his hips bucking, fighting to maintain eye contact. A low, guttural groan escaped, his jaw clenched shut, and he slicked up the space between us, his thick lashes fluttering as his mouth dropped open, soundless ...beautiful.

The sight of Michael losing control, combined with the sudden lack of friction, tipped me over the edge. Clenching thick handfuls of the pillow to either side of Michael's head, I released the tension that had been building within me since our encounter in his apartment.

Michael gasped, followed by a long sigh, and began laughing, shaking us both.

"Oh, my god." He gripped my face in his hand, demanding my attention. "Why the hell didn't we do this sooner?"

I untangled our legs and climbed off Michael, landing in an exhausted heap beside him.

"Ah ...probably because we're a couple of straight guys."

Michael turned onto his side, facing me, and set his hand on my arm. "Yeah, that would do it." He ran his fingers into my hair, and leaned over and kissed me. He only lingered for a moment before he rolled away from me onto his back.

"So, where do we go from here?" he asked.

"I have no idea."

Michael nudged my hip with his hand. "Friends with benefits?"

"Um …yeah, I guess."

God, it was so much more than that.

I could feel it in my bones. My attraction to Michael was more profound than a desire to shoot off my load with a friend.

I was willing to take what I could get, though. Suffocate my feelings so I could spend more time with Michael like this.

"So, Brenda and I went on another date a few nights ago."

"What?"

Out of left field, or what?

Michael furrowed his brow. "You know …dinner and stuff."

"And?" If Michael told me *stuff* was him and Brenda going back to his place and having sex, I was going to have to beat the crap out of him.

"And nothing. We ate dinner and went for a walk. Spent the whole time fighting about the kids." Michael heaved out a sigh. "Wasted our babysitter's time."

I stared up at the ceiling. I had been envisioning lying in bed with Michael, but now that he'd dropped that little bomb, the only thing I wanted was a shower.

"I'm going to grab a shower."

I didn't wait to hear his answer. It wasn't Michael's fault. He had no idea my emotions were heading in all sorts of dangerous directions. Friends with benefits wasn't on the list of possibilities I was carrying around in my head.

I turned on the water, replaying the brief conversation we'd just had.

Why on earth had Michael decided his ex-wife was good post-sex conversation?

"Hey." Michael wandered into the shower stall and stepped up behind me, placing his hands on my shoulders. The hot water pummeling my chest felt good.

Michael's hands felt better.

"Hey." I peered over at him.

"I get the feeling I stuck my foot in it back there." Michael dug his thumbs into the tense muscles of my neck, massaging,—driving me insane with desire for him. "I'd never sleep with you if I was back with my ex-wife."

I rolled my head side to side, enjoying the attention of Michael's hands.

"I know." I reached back and touched Michael's thigh. Taut, muscular—powerful—and they'd been wrapped around my body only moments ago. I closed my eyes, intoxicated by Michael's touch, as he embraced me in his arms and kissed the back of my ear.

"I would never do that to you, Ryan," Michael whispered, his hot breath swirling past my cheek. "Not you …never you." He tugged at the lobe of my ear with his teeth and tightened his hold on me. I trembled, nearly slipping as Michael's hard cock pressed into the small of my back.

My heart fluttered in my chest, unsure what Michael's next move would be. *It doesn't matter.* I placed my hands on the tiles in front of me. *Whatever he wants from me—I'll do it.*

Michael kissed the back of my neck, and lingered there, the tip of his nose tracing circles on my skin, his cock sliding up and down the length of my lower spine.

Up—down, up—down …until the temptation was agonizing. It was becoming difficult to breathe—hopeless to resist.

God, no, I can't.

"Michael ...," I whispered, with the intention of asking him to stop. It didn't turn out that way. The words, "I want you to take me," slipped out before I'd fully weighed their magnitude.

Michael's hands slid down to my hips. "Are you sure?"

I nodded. "There are condoms in the cupboard. Behind the towels."

I turned the water off and placed my forehead on the tiles.

How on earth did I get here?

I had been asking myself that question a lot recently.

Michael returned a few moments later and slid his hand down the length of my spine and onto my ass. "You're sure." His fingers found their way between my legs to stroke my balls. He retreated, tentative, his hesitance reminding me that we were in this together.

"I just have one question." It was something that had been rattling around in my head since the incident in Michael's apartment.

"Just one?"

I licked my lips. I was curious, nothing more. "When you were a kid hanging out with my brother at our place ...bugging me all the time ..." I gasped as Michael's finger found its target. I adjusted the stance of my legs. If I was going to do this, there was no point in being shy.

"When I was a kid ...what?" Michael chuckled in my ear, knowing damn well he'd thrown me off my train of thought.

I might as well spit it out. "Did you have a crush on me?"

Michael's hand slipped out from between my thighs. "You think that a childhood crush is what this is about for me?"

"No, but—"

"You couldn't be further from the truth. I never had a crush on you, Ryan. You were Sam's grumpy, older brother with an awesome record collection, that's it."

I spun around and placed my hand on Michael's chest. I'd offended him—the last thing I'd ever want to do. "I'm sorry." I reached up and touched his face, playing my fingers along the precise line separating his beard from his cheek. "It wouldn't matter if you had. I shouldn't have brought it up."

Michael cracked a thin smile. "Do you remember how Janice used to torture me, calling me names, shrieking at me if I dared look through the doorway of her bedroom?"

I grinned. "Yeah, Janice was pretty brutal on you, and you never said a word ..." *No.* This was beyond insane. "You had a crush on my sister?"

"I thought I did." Michael pushed me toward the far end of the shower, his open palm spread out on my chest, directing me. "But I don't want to talk about her, and I don't want to talk about my ex-wife. I'm here with you right now, and it's you, Ryan Middleton, I want."

Want.

Such a small word with so much significance.

I sucked in my next breath as Michael turned me to face the wall. He pinned me against it, pressing his forearm across my shoulders. I closed my eyes, doing my best to relax, and was launched into the most erotically, mind-altering experience of my life.

Chapter Nine

"Come here." Michael's hand touched my shoulder, drawing me to him. I'd been lying there watching him sleep, thin beams of sunlight washing him in an incredible golden hue. The rise and fall of his chest, even the soft sounds of him snoring, had brought me a great sense of peace.

It was the first time in years I'd slept the whole night through.

I rearranged the blankets after I tucked my back against Michael's chest. He folded his arm over my body and kissed the back of my head. He stayed there, humming a familiar blues tune into my hair. It made me smile. Last night we'd engaged in an act I'd never conceived of having anything to do with, and it hadn't felt the least bit awkward or *wrong*. A few laughs over missteps, a duration of pain which Michael had talked me through …then pure, bonding bliss.

I had no regrets.

"There's something I should have told you," Michael said.

Oh, god …now what?"

"I'm sorry, I really am." Michael smiled against the back of my head. "I feel terrible."

"You are terrible." I reached back and smacked his leg. "What is it? Tell me."

Michael squeezed me tight in his arms. "It was my birthday yesterday."

"Oh, my god …you are such an ass." I found Michael's hand and intertwined my fingers with his. "I thought you were going to tell me you had an STD or something."

Michael snorted, laughing. The feel of his body shaking with amusement vibrated through me, making me smile. His consistent, joyful approach was threatening to become contagious.

"Happy belated birthday." I rolled back, glancing over my shoulder at him. "How old are you anyway?" My ability to do math had been successfully pounded out of me in the shower the night before. Not that I minded in the least. I'd never liked math.

"Twenty-nine."

I shifted uncomfortably in Michael's arms. I knew there was an eight-year age difference between us, but having that difference put Michael in the twenty's category hadn't dawned on me for some reason. Which was stupid. Michael was the same age as my little brother.

"Is that a problem?"

I laughed aloud. A deep, cleansing, hearty laugh. What else could I do?

I pulled myself out of Michael's arms, rolled and flung my leg over his body, straddling his hips. There was so much more I wanted to explore with this man.

His age had nothing to do with it.

Michael smiled up at me, running his hands across my chest and down to my abs. "What's got your funny bone tweaking, all out of character?"

My source of amusement…

Despite every argument I'd had with myself over the past few weeks about following my head instead of my heart, I'd become inextricably hooked on my baby brother's best friend.

And judging by the way Michael had come at me in the front entry, the bedroom, the shower, …and again in the bedroom, he was pretty ensnared as well.

I slid down Michael's body, kissing his neck, his collarbone, then brushed my cheek and lips through the coarse hair on his chest. He smelled of soap, perspiration, and sex. I shoved the blankets out of my way so I could continue my exploration.

Michael's stomach trembled beneath my lips.

It gave me a heady rush.

"In a roundabout way, I was thinking about how Sam would be absolutely horrified if he found out about this." I lay a single kiss on each of Michael's hipbones.

He squirmed, groaning, his cock lengthening.

I chewed at my bottom lip, containing an all-out sigh of exhilaration.

It made me smile, the connection we'd formed with each other. The power we had over one another. I ran my lips along the length of Michael's cock and looked up at him.

"Let's leave him out of this, shall we?" Michael pushed his hand into my hair and grasped a handful of it. I extended the tip of my tongue, testing the taste and feel of the tightening cap beneath my lips. A few small circles left me wanting more.

Unfortunately, a crash followed by a thud, and the sound of excited children shattered any plans I'd had of driving Michael to more places that were new to us.

"Shit, what time is it?" I scrambled to the head of the bed and reached for my phone.

Nine-thirty.

My forehead creased as I searched my mind for the reason Janice was dropping the kids off early. Usually, she kept them until eleven.

The third Sunday of the month.

Janice had her ladies auxiliary meeting to go to this morning.

Michael gathered the blankets around his waist as he sat up. "What do you want me to do?" Before I had a chance to answer, a knock came on the door.

"Ryan, are you awake?" Janice sounded frustrated. "I phoned and left a ton of messages reminding you about my meeting." A long pause.

During the night, I'd muted my phone, not wanting to be disturbed.

"Did we lock the door after we went downstairs for snacks?" Michael whispered.

"Unlikely. You had me crazy distracted." I grinned at him. He made a stupid face back at me, which nearly unhinged me. It was all we could do not to burst out laughing like a couple of kids.

"Ryan, I'm coming in." The handle turned freely.

Nope, we hadn't locked the door. I shoved Michael off the edge of the bed, and he barely managed to slip into the bathroom before Janice opened the bedroom door.

Janice stepped into the bedroom, both hands on her hips. She perused the room briefly, wrinkled up her nose, and looked at me. The sound of water in the bathroom had her looking in that direction. It was then she saw Michael's obviously male articles of clothing hanging indiscriminately off the antique smoking chair Rebecca had picked up during college.

"Ryan, I think we need to talk."

I gathered the top sheet around me as I climbed out of bed. Michael had dragged the blanket with him halfway to the bathroom. "Okay but let me put some clothes on first." I held the door open for Janice as I ushered her into the hallway. "Can you do me a favor and keep the kids in the family room until my guest has left? Then we can talk."

Janice grunted an acceptance of sorts and headed for the

stairs. This was going to take a lot of explaining. The only heartening talisman of sorts, a long, sensuous kiss from Michael before he absconded down the stairs carrying a sworn oath that I'd call him.

If Janice didn't kill me first.

"Then explain it to me. Explain to me why there were men's clothes scattered all over your bedroom." Janice spun to face me. The coffee pot had only started brewing the fluid that was going to be my life's blood for the next few hours.

There was no way I was going to wiggle out of this.

Yet, I decided to try anyway.

"I was going through my closet. The clothes are mine."

Janice slammed her hand down on the kitchen counter. "Bullshit. You don't own clothes that nice. And what bank did you knock over to get your hands on those shoes and that cologne?"

"Fine." I slid onto one of the barstools. "Just keep your voice down." I looked out through the sliding glass doors. The kids were playing happily on the swing set in their snowsuits.

Janice leaned forward, resting her arms on the counter across from me.

"Well …?"

"Okay, you're right, I had someone over last night …a *guy* someone."

"Since when …" Janice stood and crossed her arms. I could see the revulsion wash over her expression. I hadn't expected that. "A man …?"

"Last I checked, yeah, and I checked twice this morning, and three times last night." I know I shouldn't have worded my reply that way, but the last thing I'd expected walking into this conversation was that my sister was a homophobe.

"Fuck, Ryan …" Janice turned from me and headed for the kitchen sink. She turned on the water, letting in run. "Who is it?"

"I'm not telling you that."

"Please tell me it isn't Michael," she whispered as she shut the tap off.

"It isn't Michael," I responded flatly. She knew I was lying. Her hand was clamped over her mouth when she turned around.

"How could you?"

"How could I what, Janice?"

"Mikey …that's Sam's Mikey."

"Yes, I occasionally remember that, but most of the time, not. Michael is nothing like the Mikey who used to run around our house with Sam."

Janice made a coughing, choking sound. "I should hope not."

I slipped off my stool and headed for the coffee pot. This was going to require copious amounts of caffeine. Janice was settling in at the dining room table.

"Coffee?"

Janice nodded, her hands clasped, poised at her lips. "Please."

I was not expecting the next question she fired at me, although I should have seen it coming.

"You didn't touch him back then, did you?"

I smashed my cup down, spilling hot coffee everywhere. "That's where your mind went? That I was a pedophile because I shared my bed with someone I knew when he was a kid." I grabbed a cloth, attempting to mop up the mess I'd made.

What the hell are you doing?

I didn't owe my sister an explanation.

I pitched the cloth at the sink and turned to face her.

"Michael and I are both adults, Janice. I can attest to that in graphic detail." I crossed my arms, clutching at the fabric of my undershirt.

There was that inflammatory language again. My sister had shaken me up.

Janice jumped to her feet. "I'm sorry. That came out all wrong." She wrapped her arms around me and hugged me. I decided to let her, eventually breaking down and hugging her back.

"That hurt, Janice."

"I know, I'm sorry. I was just wondering if any of this is because of some attraction you had for each other back then."

"No, of course not." I stepped back from her embrace. She needed to see the sincerity in my eyes. "Michael and I have really connected since we ran into each other. That's it. He's my best friend, and for some reason, we ended up on this collision course with each other."

Janice sat back down at the table. I set her coffee in front of her. Three sugars, no milk.

"But sleeping with him, Ryan ..." Janice stared up at me. I pulled out a chair and sat beside her. "Are you in a relationship with him?'

"No, it's nothing like that." Even though I wished it was. "Just a couple of buddies getting each other off, that's it."

Janice took a sip of her coffee. "I don't understand that. If you're so desperate for sex, Amy seems up for it ...from what you've told me."

"It's not the same thing. Michael and I have a connection."

"Yes, you've said that ..." Janice peered into my eyes. "Do you have feelings for him?"

"No, and don't go there." I drained my cup and retreated to

the kitchen. "It's a weird chemistry thing, I don't know. He showed up here yesterday, looking like he did, all dressed up for that wedding ..." I ran my fingers across my lips, remembering the feel of Michael's on mine. "We both lost it. Jumped each other in the front hall."

Janice stepped up behind me. "Was last night the first time? Or was your fight a result of something similar?"

I sighed and headed for the dishwasher, placing my cup inside. I don't know why I was even considering opening up to my sister about this. Perhaps because I'd always trusted her judgment. Or maybe I just needed someone to talk to.

"I was embarrassed, Janice. What we did together at his apartment scared me. Somewhere in the back of my mind, I'd assumed it would feel wrong. But it didn't feel wrong. In fact, it felt incredibly right. So much so, I ran out of there in the middle of the night."

Janice wrinkled her brow. "Maybe you're gay."

I hadn't even considered that. Rebecca had been the entirety of my experience when it came to romantic relationships. I didn't know anything else. My love for her had been so profound, perhaps it had overshadowed my sexual desire for men.

I scrubbed a hand across my face. No, our sex life had been full and beautiful. I loved everything about women; their soft curves, delicate limbs—their velvety pink nipples...

My cock stirred.

Yeah, not gay.

"No, pretty sure I'm not."

"And Michael?"

I blinked and furrowed my brow. "No idea. Maybe he is, maybe he isn't. I don't really care."

Janice lifted a plum to her mouth and tore off a small piece.

She leaned against the counter near the sink. "Walk me through this."

"Through what?" I reached past her and turned on the tap to wash my hands. I'd run my hand through some honey residue on the dining room table. I dried them on the tea towel hanging from the oven door.

"When you see Michael, what do you see?"

"Seriously?"

"Yeah, big brother, seriously. I want to understand what you see in him."

"I don't know." I sighed and crossed my arms. "Like I said, we've become good friends. He's intelligent, carefree, and funny. All of which have been good for me. We're both passionate about the blues, and he's created an incredible career out of it. I respect him for that."

I stuffed my hands into the pockets of my jeans. "He's crazy talented. He listens when I drone on about Rebecca. He's patient. And he's crazy about his kids. Michael is an awesome dad." I smiled. "He was able to handle the entire brood of them, his and mine, like a pro."

Janice blinked and looked at the floor. "And what about the physical stuff?"

I propelled myself across the kitchen, heading for the fridge. Before I opened it, I took a moment, resting my hand on the handle. "Firstly, Michael is gorgeous." I turned to face Janice. "Especially those eyes of his ...and those damn lashes." I watched for verification from Janice, as if I needed some kind of confirmation that I wasn't losing my mind.

"Sure, yeah." Janice nodded. "If it weren't Mikey, I wouldn't throw him out of bed."

I smirked. "Yeah, me either, until you decided to open my

bedroom door. I had to send him scrambling for the bathroom."

I licked my lips, the feel of Michael's hands on me in the shower last night, still so fresh in my mind. Rocking—thrusting, pounding me into the wall.

"There's something incredibly virile about him." I remained with one foot still in that memory, speaking as if no one were listening. "His body, so strong, so seductive. So commanding."

I sighed and leaned against the fridge for support. I was in deeper than I'd realized. "And Michael's lips …fuck. The taste of them, the feel of them on mine. Trailing down my body—"

"Okay, stop." Janice shoved me in the chest, breaking me from the memory. "I've heard enough. I wanted to make sure Michael wasn't coercing you somehow." She patted me on the back. "Just looking out for you, big bro, but you are totally sunk."

I looked up at the ceiling. "I'm in trouble, aren't I?"

"That is the understatement of the century." Janice leaned in and kissed my cheek. "I'll see you tomorrow morning when I pick up the kids."

"Yeah." I nodded. "Thanks, sis. And, please …don't tell anyone about this, all right?"

"Who would I tell? This is between you and Michael. And I think you both know Sam would never forgive you for this. He's known Michael since he was five." Janice set her hand on my shoulder. "You were a teenager when Michael was in kindergarten, Ryan. Think about that for a minute. I suggest you get this out of your system quick and move on before someone gets hurt."

I knew Janice was right, but it wasn't that easy. I returned the hug she offered and waved at her as she made her way to the front entry. When I heard the front door close, I wandered over to the sofa and collapsed into it. I only managed to get two minutes of peace before a tumble of three monkey children spilled in from outside and into my arms.

"How did it go?" Michael's baritone voice carried through the phone like a comfortable blanket I'd misplaced at some point in my life, having only just discovered it again recently.

"She knows. I had to tell Janice everything. She pretty much figured it out on her own."

"She isn't going to tell Sam, is she?"

"No, of course not."

Michael sighed. "I'm sorry."

"About what? You didn't do anything wrong." I scrubbed a hand through my hair. He was making me nervous. Maybe Michael thought we had done something wrong. Maybe last night was a one-time thing. I didn't know if I could handle that, not being able to touch him again.

"I can hear your mind whirring all the way out in Denver." The sound of rustling sheets. It had taken a while to get the kids into bed tonight. It was late.

"And what are the whirring sounds telling you?"

"That you're worried I'm going to abscond on you now that we've consummated this benefits package we have going on. Which would kind of defeat the purpose, wouldn't it?"

Benefits package?

That cut deep. I thought we'd made more of a connection than that.

"Yeah, something like that," I said finally.

"Ryan, buddy, I'm not going anywhere. Best friends, remember."

"Yeah." I slid down in bed, exhausted, and apparently delusional if I thought Michael was going to be anything more than a best friend with benefits.

Janice had spoken the truth. Someone *was* going to end up getting hurt.

It would most likely be me.

The rest of our conversation was awkward after that. My heart wasn't in it, and for the first time in weeks, I didn't fall asleep imaging Michael's arms around me.

My phone lit up, buzzing, alerting me to a text message. I looked at the screen. It was two-twenty in the morning. The words, *are you up*, had me sitting up in bed.

I typed *maybe* and threw the phone onto the covers beside me. The next sound was my phone ringing. I answered it quickly, not wanting it to wake the kids.

"Hey, Michael," I whispered. "What is it?"

"I couldn't sleep."

"Obviously."

"No, I mean, I need to talk to you."

I sighed, unsure if I wanted to launch into a conversation with Michael. It was late, I was still hurting from his earlier comment, and I'd only just fallen asleep. "About what?"

"I was lying here thinking I needed to talk to someone about what happened last night. The only problem is, you're the only person I want to share this with. You're the only person who understands why we ended up where we are. You're the only person who can explain why I felt so cold and alone when I crawled into bed tonight."

"Fuck, Michael." I threw my covers off. "You have no idea how glad I am you said that. I would give anything to have you back here in bed with me."

"I'd drive out there, but I have a session booked for six in the morning." Michael sighed. "Ryan, how is this going to work between us? Only seeing you every second weekend when my wife has the kids is not going to work for me. Every time I close my eyes, I can feel your hands on me." An audible groan carried through the phone.

"So much more than that, actually," Michael added. "Damn, Ryan, I had no idea you'd feel so good. I'll never be able to have a shower again without remembering what it felt like to be inside you." A short shuddering gasp followed. "Gawd, I think I've made things worse."

"You and me both." I stroked the palm of my hand along the outline of my stiffening cock through my pajama bottom. "Seriously, what *are* we going to do? I somehow doubt Janice will be open to watching the kids so I can drive to Denver to hook up with you."

Michael was silent for much longer than was typical for him.

"Michael?"

"Sorry, I was just wondering about something."

"What?"

"It's nothing. I'm just tired."

"Tell me, anyway."

Michael exhaled, clearly unsure. "Is that all we're doing …hooking up? I can't shake the feeling it might be more than that. That's why you were upset with me earlier, right? It was the *benefits package* comment. As soon as it left my mouth, it didn't feel right."

"It did sound a bit cold." I scrubbed a hand across my face. There was only one solution if we were going to make this work. Knowing Michael was thinking beyond having a strictly *benefits package* arrangement changed everything. "Michael, how soon can you be here tomorrow night?"

"I'm not sure. It might be a long day, …maybe nine? Let me check." The ambient sound in Michael's bedroom changed. He'd put me on speakerphone while he was checking his schedule.

"Tick-tick-tick-tick …" I grinned, knowing I'd filled his bedroom with sound. I was rewarded with one of Michael's contagious snorting laughs.

"Cut it out," he cried, still laughing. "I'm trying to figure this out. Right—okay. Yup …nope, wait. Okay. Yes, …I can finish by seven."

"Perfect." Seventeen hours from now, Michael would be back with me.

"Wait, what about the kids, Ryan?"

"You can help me tuck them in if they're still awake."

A brief moment of silence. "Are you sure that's a good idea?"

"The kids think you're great, Michael. And you said it yourself, we're doing more than hooking up. This isn't a booty call. I want to hang out with you first. Maybe have dinner, listen to some music. The kids will never know you stuck around long after they went to bed."

"True …but still."

"Still what? We'll have a nice evening together. The only difference being we'll crawl into bed for a few hours before you go home."

"Like an old married couple …minus the driving home part."

"Ha, ha …very funny." I smoothed the bedding out beside me, recalling the image of Michael asleep beside me. I needed him back with me. "Does that make you uncomfortable, my wanting something a little less casual?"

"No. Not at all. I'd be lying if I said I didn't want the same thing."

"Then it's settled? I'll see you around seven-thirty?"

"We can divide and conquer the bedtime routine, then order in some Chinese. Maybe watch a movie. How does that sound?"

Michael had read my mind.

"Exactly the kind of night I'm craving."

"Is that all you're craving?"

I laughed. "You know it's not. Now go to sleep." I pulled the covers up and lay back down. "I'll see you tonight."

Sleep came easier this time. I knew where I stood with Michael. We had a plan. One that combined our friendship with this whole new aspect of physical connection.

I grinned into my pillow. Life was beginning to make sense again.

Chapter Ten

Michael had driven out to Longmont almost every night this week. Arriving in the evening and leaving in the middle of the night. Not ideal, but I loved having him around to tackle the evening routine with me. And the kids were ecstatic about having Uncle Mike read them bedtime stories. He had a knack for creating and remembering wacky voices for every character in their books.

Twice, Michael had arrived just after dinner, thrilling the kids. Those longer evenings were somewhat agonizing, only being able to grab small snatches of time in back hallways and washrooms for ourselves. Anywhere out of range of prying eyes. Furtive kisses and hands reacquainting themselves without any possibility of release until the children were in bed.

But after that—pure bliss.

All the driving, though...

Michael was exhausted, and his work was suffering.

It was unsustainable, and we both knew it.

Unfortunately, I'd been correct in assuming Janice would refuse to watch the kids if I planned to drive into Denver for an overnight visit to *bang my buddy*.

Her words, not mine.

We'd tried late night *sexy* phone calls, but those typically ended up with both of us laughing ourselves into convulsions. This was one of those times.

"This is ridiculous. I'm driving out to see you."

"You can't, Michael."

"It's Christmas next week. I can close the studio for the holidays. Rebook everyone in after the end of the holidays. I can spend the entire weekend with you and our crazy brood of kids."

"Sounds relaxing."

"You want relaxing? I can draw you a bath after the kids go to bed." Michael laughed softly. "Then proceed to ravish you in it."

A surge of willpower-disabling lust reached my cock. The last time we'd been in the bathtub, I'd been straddling Michael, water sloshing rhythmically onto the floor as I rode him.

My nipples tightened, recalling the pinch of his fingers on them as I'd cum in the bathwater.

"I changed my mind." I reached beneath the sheets and stroked the length of my cock. "How soon can you be here?"

Sometime in the last twenty-four hours, our *friends with benefits* agreement had completely dissolved like a well-intentioned container of ice left out on a hot summer day.

Now it was just us. So wrapped up in one another, it was becoming difficult to not see this for what it was for me. Our connection with each other had become absolute—fast.

Thirty minutes later, Michael was on my doorstep, and his mouth was on mine before I had a chance to ask how fast he'd been driving.

We crashed onto the bed, fully clothed.

There would be plenty of time to strip each other bare.

Plenty of time to test each other's endurance before the night was through.

Michael took first initiative, sitting up to remove my pajama bottoms. He released my cock to the cool air and shuffled down the bed, hands gripping my hips, his chest resting on my thighs.

Without using his hands, Michael licked a slick, wet path along my shaft, humming as he continued dragging his tongue up and down along its length—tasting, savoring.

He was beautiful.

Looking down at him, watching him—Michael took my breath away.

I groaned, enthralled by the entire scene. This beautiful man in my bed, sharing our bodies, possessing each other in ways I'd never dreamed possible.

The perfection of it nearly brought me to tears.

I gripped the sheets tightly as Michael wrapped his hand around my shaft and pulled my foreskin tight to my body, exposing the thick-ridged head. His tongue dipped into the slit, teasing and infuriating it, each flick of his tongue testing my ability to stay quiet.

We'd become fastidious about locking the bedroom door, but there had been times when one or both of us had barely managed to contain the grunts and groans of cumming hard.

It was unnerving. I'd never cum as hard as when I was with Michael. Not ever. There was something about this man that drove my body wild.

Michael traveled back up until he reached my mouth. His lips met mine, and I forgot about everything. Everything except my intensifying feelings for him.

I stroked my fingers through Michael's hair and pulled away from his lips.

"Undress for me."

Michael smirked and removed himself from the bed.

I rolled onto my side to watch him. Michael's abs, pecs, and broad shoulders were revealed first as he pulled his shirt off over his head—ever so slowly. The clink of his silver buckle, the wide, black leather belt dragged free of his pants, loop by agonizing loop.

The button—the zipper.

"Take them off." I reached for Michael, but he stepped out of reach of my roving, outstretched hand. He turned away from me and slowly stripped his pants and designer underwear off his gorgeous ass, giving me the view of a lifetime.

"Enough." I grinned at Michael as he turned to face me. "Get back over here." I made quick work of my t-shirt as he stretched out on the bed.

The fact he'd readied me early in the game meant he wanted only one thing. I slid open the bedside drawer and grabbed a condom and some lube. I shook the bottle. It would need to be replaced soon. Our antics seemed to require an abundance of lubrication.

Michael adjusted his legs and wrapped them around my waist as I pressed into him. He groaned; his hands gripping my head, his forehead pressed to mine. The urge to plunge into him hard and fast, tempered only by my escalating affection for him.

More.

So much more.

I tasted Michael's lips, then withdrew to watch him. He was exquisite, gasping and sighing beneath me, begging me to go deeper, his thick lashes fluttering in ecstasy—

My emotions overwhelmed me.

I'd done it.

I knew it without question.

I pressed my eyes closed to keep the tears I'd been shedding for nights from forming. I'd fallen in love with Michael

Sanderson.

And it terrified me.

I don't know when it happened. All I know is that before Michael arrived tonight, I'd felt compelled to slip my wedding ring off and place it in a small box, destined for a space in the back of my dresser. An area I'd dedicated to some of Rebecca's smaller things.

I was scared to death what that meant.

I opened my eyes and fixed them on Michael's. Right now, for these few hours, he was with me, feeling the full force of my love for him. Whether he realized it or not, it didn't matter.

Michael knew I cared profoundly for him.

That would need to be enough.

"Ryan," Michael whispered. "Where did you go?"

"Nowhere." I smiled down at Michael and kissed him. "I'm right here with you."

Michael wrapped his arms around me and hugged me to him. "I need you tonight, Ryan. I need you to be here with me."

"I am." I kissed Michael again and thrust my hips hard against the flesh of his thighs, burying my cock high inside him. He grunted and adjusted his hips, taking me in deeper.

"Yeah, right there," he whispered.

I adjusted my position, hooking my arms under Michael's legs, then leaned into him, lifting his ass clear off the bedding. "Ready?" I whispered against Michael's lips.

"Always." Michael's hand stroked my face, then he kissed me. A long, sensuous, mind-decimating kiss. The kind that made you forget your name.

It was soon upon Michael's lips as he cried out for me, pleading—whimpering, and clawing at my shoulders as I sank into him.

Michael wanted a pummeling, and I was predictably impatient to oblige him. Any feelings I had for him would have to entertain themselves for the time being.

Michael grabbed hold of my hand as we tripped our way into the dimly lit kitchen, laughing and shushing each other like a couple of kids. He didn't let go of me, even after we'd safely arrived at the counter, instead pulling me to him and kissing the life out of me.

Tongue seeking, hand caressing, annihilation.

He'd reduced my muscles to porridge by the time he was done with me. I had to cling to him when he released me to ensure I didn't end up in a puddle on the floor at his feet.

"Damn, I hate when you do that." I wrapped my arms around Michael's waist and laid a sensuous kiss on his collarbone. The bristles of his beard tickled my ear.

It made me smile.

Those same bristles had been caressing the inside of my thighs only moments before.

"I can tell. You go all quiet and almost fall down." Michael leaned back, lifted my face, and gave me a soft, breathy kiss. "Ice cream," he said against my lips. "We came down for ice cream."

"Right." I groaned, reluctant to leave Michael's embrace as he turned me away from him and nudged me toward the fridge. I had to dig for the container of Triple Chunk. It was hidden at the back, so the kids wouldn't find it.

It had become a ritual, standing in the glow of the kitchen's nightlight, snacking on whatever I had handy before Michael left to make the long trek home.

It didn't take long until Michael's ice cream coated lips found mine, spiraling me back into a fog. I tossed my spoon into the sink with a clatter.

Who needed a spoon when I had these lips to feed me?

"Dad?"

Shit.

I spun around. "Taylor, what are you doing up?"

"I was thirsty."

"Thirsty?" Michael waggled his spoon in the air. "That's easy to fix. You're lucky. We needed ice cream." He jammed his spoon into the ice cream, set the container on the counter, and ruffled Taylor's hair affectionately before heading to the cupboard to retrieve Taylor's sports bottle.

It was different when Michael did it, tousled Taylor's hair. Taylor never fussed the way he did with me. Of course, he wouldn't. Uncle Mike was cool, unlike his boring dad.

Water in hand, Taylor climbed up onto a stool facing the kitchen island. "Uncle Mike, why do you keep leaving in the middle of the night?"

"Um, …well." Michael scratched at his beard. "I have to get home …to get some sleep."

"So you can go to work."

Michael pointed at Taylor. "Exactly."

Taylor took a sip of water, his mind obviously mulling over his next question.

"Do you like kissing my dad?"

Michael nearly choked on his spoonful of ice cream. He dragged the back of his hand across his lips to clear the sticky residue. "You caught that."

"Kind of hard to miss."

"Well, your dad and I, we—"

"You like each other," Taylor finished for Michael.

"That sounds about right." I reached for Michael, settled my arm around his waist, and tugged him to me. We'd talked about keeping our arrangement a secret from the kids, the fact that Uncle Mike was sleeping over with their dad. We hadn't come to any decisions yet, but it seemed our cover was blown. It had only been a matter of time.

"Taylor, look—" I started.

"It's okay, Dad, I know Uncle Mike stays for sleepovers."

"Do you now?"

Taylor sighed. "I don't see what the big deal is. You're lonely. I get it." With that, my eldest son removed himself from the kitchen and headed for the stairs.

"Okay, that was unexpected," Michael whispered against my ear, smiling. "Are you sure that kid of yours is only eleven?"

"Positive." I glanced at the clock. It was two-eighteen in the morning. Michael was only going to manage four hours of sleep before he had to head into work. He needed the break he'd been talking about. "So, this weekend. The whole weekend. You'll pack up the kids and head out here."

Michael smirked at me. "Does that excite you, Ryan?"

"Perhaps." I wrapped my arms around Michael's waist, swaying in time to a song that had popped into my head. I hummed a few bars of the song, and Michael's eyes lit up.

"B.B. King's *Waitin' on You.*"

"You're good." I patted Michael's chest. "But do you know the lyrics."

"Easy." Michael pulled me into the family room to sit with him on the sofa.

I curled up in one corner, feet tucked up, prepared to be entertained. Michael's ability to remember lyrics was stunning. And if he couldn't remember them, he made them up.

Typically, a bawdy variety of lyrics if we were alone.

We'd all been privy to some of Michael's less polished vocals over the past few evenings, along with some professionally stunning renditions of both jazz and blues classics. My favorite, his comedic interpretation of Lena Horne's *Stormy Weather*. The kids however, had preferred his Led Zeppelin classic rock imitations, screaming and leaping around in time to the music.

"*Yes, it's four o'clock in the morning, baby ...,*" Michael started singing.

I snorted out a laugh. He was going to pull this one-off. In true Michael Sanderson fashion, he was going to pull this off.

Michael grinned at me and started again.

"*Yes, it's four o'clock in the morning, baby. I'm sitting here waiting on you.*

Yes, it's four o'clock in the morning, baby. I'm sitting here waiting on you.

Yeah, you say you're going out dancing. But the dance hall closes at two."

"Not bad ...not bad. Keep going."

"Oh, come one ..."

"Keep going, Michael, or there will be no more ice cream for you."

"But there's something I want more than ice cream."

I shoved the side of Michael's leg with my foot. "Then, keep going."

Michael rolled his eyes.

"*Yes, I know it's the weekend, mama. And everybody's having fun.*

Yes, I know it's the weekend, mama. And everybody's having fun.

But when it's time for loving, baby. Remember, I'm the only one."

Michael winked at me and reached for my hand. "You know you are."

"And yet, it's still nice to hear you say it."

"Or sing it, apparently."

I squeezed Michael's hand and pulled myself over to sit at his end of the sofa, cuddling up against him, my head on his shoulder. I had something serious I wanted to bring up with him.

"Earlier, when we were in bed, you said you *needed* me tonight. That you *needed me to be here* with you. What did you mean by that?"

"I said that?"

"You know you did."

"You're my safe place, Ryan. Surely, you know that. I needed you to be fully present." Michael sighed and looked up at the ceiling. "Brenda has been on my case. I haven't been answering her phone calls lately. Mainly because I've been hanging out here with you."

"I don't understand." I sat up and touched Michael's face. His beautiful eyes had changed from glistening emerald to muddy green. Something was wrong. "What about the situation with Brenda has you climbing into my bed seeking solace?"

"She's insane."

"That's old news, Michael."

Michael tightened his grip on me. "She wants us to get back together."

"What?" I stroked my hand across Michael's stomach, hoping to soothe my own from erupting into my throat. "That's not even a possibility, is it?"

"Of course not." Michael kissed the top of my head. "She just gets to me. Always coming at me with something." He touched my chin, tipping my face to look at him. "You're the only thing other than the kids, and my music, that makes any sense in my life."

Michael kissed my lips. "You ground me. I needed that from you tonight."

"Who knew? This best friend stuff is hard." I grinned at him. "A man crawling into my bed at all hours of the night, begging me to fuck them until they forget their ex-wives."

And just like that, Michael's eyes lit up again.

The ensuing shrieking and squealing couldn't be contained. Apparently, I had no willpower when it came to gorgeous men like Michael tickling me.

Chapter Eleven

Friday came and went without any word from Michael. He'd promised to call and figure out a time for him and his kids to arrive at my place on Saturday. Sleeping arrangements had been made, the kids were beyond excited, and my fridge was stocked to overflowing, but I hadn't seen or heard from Michael since Thursday night when he'd assured me everything was all right—since the night he'd told me I was one of the few things in his life that made sense.

I knew Michael was okay because his texts were showing as read. He just wasn't replying to them. The uncertainty of what might be happening was scrambling my brain. I suspected it had to do with Michael's ex-wife, but to what extent she was going to come between us, I had no idea.

What I did know ...two days without Michael was too much.

A light tapping on my front door sent me leaping to my feet.

"Hey," Michael whispered as I hauled the door open. He looked beleaguered as though he'd been fighting for his life. When I moved to kiss him, Michael grabbed my shoulders and stopped me.

My stomach dropped.

This was it. When Michael hadn't texted me back right away, I'd sensed it coming but convinced myself I was being paranoid.

I braced myself, leaning against the nearest wall as Michael closed the door behind him. He stared at me, his expression almost cold, seemingly prepared to rip my heart out.

I wanted to reach for him. His usually expressive eyes were bloodshot, distant, and glazed.

He'd been crying.

"Where have you been, Michael? I've been calling?"

"I'm sorry." Michael closed his eyes and steadied his breath. "I didn't call you back because you deserve to hear this from me in person. This was the soonest I could drive out here."

"It's over. Isn't it?"

Michael simply nodded.

"Why?" I breathed easier as Michael held out his hand for me, even though I knew it would be short-lived. I attempted to memorize the exact feel of his grip as he led me into the living room.

We sank onto the sofa together.

"Brenda and I …"

Please, no.

Hearing Michael use his ex-wife's name in conjunction with himself made me cringe. Knowing she may have touched Michael before he'd come here sent razor blades down my spine.

Up until a couple of nights ago, Michael had been mine.

All mine.

He'd told me I was the only one.

Liar.

I yanked my hand from Michael's grasp.

"Ryan …"

"No, it's all right. It's what's best for the kids."

"Is it?" Michael covered his face and leaned back. "I'm moving into the house with her and the kids on Christmas Eve." He crossed his arms, refusing to make eye contact with me. "Being able to tuck the kids into their own beds at night is a dream come true. But sharing my life and a bed with Brenda is going to be brutal …foreign—agonizing." He closed his eyes and shook his head. "I'll be all right, I suppose. Eventually. I managed well enough while we were married."

My hands clenched into fists. "Why are you telling me this? I don't want to hear about your sleeping arrangements with your ex-wife! Two nights ago, you were in my bed. In my arms."

Fuck.

A streak of tears spilled down my cheek. I'd been fighting to contain them, along with my anger. I scrubbed the mess away with the heel of my hand. I'd failed on both counts.

"I wish I still was," Michael whispered.

I turned to look at him. I needn't have been worried about my own tears. Michael was in worse shape than me. I reached for his arm.

"Michael …" I slipped my hand into his. "Baby, please. Look at me."

Michael sighed but glanced up at me. Fresh tears spilled down his face. "I'm so sorry, Ryan." He squeezed tight to my hand. "Please don't hate me."

Fuck, he's beautiful.

Even like this, distraught and dismantled, Michael took my breath away.

"I don't. I could never—" I pinched the bridge of my nose. I could never hate Michael, but maybe if I'd told him I was in love with him, this wouldn't be happening.

It was too late for all that now.

"I didn't have a choice, Ryan. She kept pushing. I ended up telling her everything about us. I was trying to get her off my back, but she threatened to file for full custody of the kids."

"She can't do that. She doesn't have a case, Michael."

Michael shook his head. "She's a lawyer. I can't take that

chance." His damp lashes concealed his gorgeous eyes—eyes I would never have the opportunity to become lost in again. They fluttered open. "Ryan, please try to understand why I had to do this."

Right now, Michael needed me to accept his decision. He'd gone back to his wife because he loved his kids with a passion that mirrored my own. Enough to place himself in a relationship that didn't make sense. A relationship that was a lie.

I nodded my head.

There was no point in arguing with him.

Michael rose to his feet. "I have to go. I promised Brenda I'd take the kids to the park."

I followed him to the front entry.

"Michael, before you go…" I needed one more. One more kiss to imprint on my memory. One more chance to be drawn into his eyes.

Michael's hands swept up onto my face, and our lips met. The kiss was aggressive and desperate, a true parting of friends—friends who had become so much more.

And then he was gone.

Michael's exit left me a weeping mess, crumpling to the floor in tears after he closed the door and walked out of my life.

It was Christmas Eve in three days, and I'd be expected to partake as if my heart hadn't been broken, because no one, not even Janice knew how much pain I'd opened myself up to.

I curled up into a ball.

Two massive holes now hung side by side, my heart torn to shreds.

Chapter Twelve

My parents' house during our annual Christmas Eve dinner was everything you'd expect it to be. An abundance of greenery, tinsel, and sparkling lights, and the aromatic smells of homemade cookies, pies, and succulent turkey, which my mom always cooked to perfection.

Every year, my mom tried to make Christmas Eve special for her grandchildren. Especially since they'd lost their mom. Rebecca had loved Christmas and always went all out decorating the house and making the entire season a memorable event for our kids.

This year was supposed to have been memorable as well. I'd thought Michael and I would be spending all of Christmas together. His ex-wife would've had Mandy and Michael Jr. until noon on Christmas Day, but once she'd dropped them off at Michael's, we'd planned to spend the remainder of Christmas and the day after with all five kids, taking in the Christmas light displays in the neighborhood, doing a bit of sledding, weather permitting, playing board games, and putting ourselves into hot chocolate and Christmas movie induced comas.

I shut my eyes, willing any tears to keep their presence to themselves. I didn't need anyone asking questions. I'd spent the last three days since Michael left hiding out in my bedroom whenever possible, only emerging when the kids were awake.

I tucked myself further into the sofa, sipping on my rum and eggnog.

The kids were busy with Sam, who'd dug through a pile of our old board games to find the well-used Game of Life. He'd managed to keep them occupied for the past hour, relieving me of any parenting duties, which I'd become delinquent in of late. I was finding it impossible to garner any enthusiasm to manage the kids with any creativity whatsoever.

I sighed and drained my glass. I'd need another drink if I was going to get through this night. I kept imagining Michael in his ex-wife's house, his belongings being placed around her space, his clothes hung beside hers in the closet. He would be moving in with her today.

I pressed the heel of my hand against my forehead, another headache building. I'd been checking my phone every ten minutes on the off-chance I'd hear from Michael. I knew it was ridiculous. He'd gone back to his old life, leaving me to gather up the remnants of my heart.

I looked around the room at my family. Michael and I had planned to come here together—as friends. To share a meal with everyone I'd come to love in my life.

I scrubbed my hand across my lips. Coming to terms with the fact I'd fallen in love with Michael had been difficult, but then losing him before I'd had a chance to tell him had destroyed me. I wasn't recovering. Every moment of every day, I had a sense of drowning I couldn't shake.

It would be a while before I could surface again.

"Hey, dinner is almost ready." Janice sat down beside me and lay her hand on my arm. " I hate seeing you like this. Is there anything I can do to help?"

I patted her hand. I appreciated how concerned my sister was for me. It made a nice change from when we were kids running around this very house. When she'd rather spit at me than look at me, her brooding, boring big brother. Time, age, and the crippling loss of Rebecca in our lives had changed our relationship for the better. Janice and I had never been closer, especially since her husband never seemed to be around for anything, including tonight's dinner.

Still, I'd chosen to exclude her.

"I just need some time." I hadn't filled Janice in on the relationship that had developed between Michael and me. That I'd fallen in love with him. That he'd broken my heart. She no doubt suspected something to that effect because she hadn't pushed me for details as to why I had gone from giddy and exuberant to despondent overnight.

Sam wandered in and perched himself on the arm of the sofa. "Yeah, bro. What the hell is going on with you? I haven't seen you like this since Rebecca died."

"Sam ..." Janice glared at our little brother. It wasn't his fault. He'd never had much empathy for other people. One of the reasons he'd found it easy to take off into the woods for years at a time, never contacting his family, despite how concerned we'd told him we were.

I shook my head. "Honestly, I'll be fine."

"Sounds good to me." Sam took off for the kitchen, presumably to grab another stack of sugar cookies. My little brother was a bottomless pit. Understandably. He'd dropped a lot of weight during his latest stint in the Colorado Rockies. At least thirty pounds. Apparently, the fishing hadn't been good, and big game had been hard to find. He'd been surviving on hares and any other rodents he came across. Seeing Sam so thin had brought my mom to tears, time and again.

"Dinner," my dad barked from his place at the head of the dining room table. My dad, gruff to a fault, but tender-hearted. I smiled at him as I approached my place.

"How are you doing, Dad."

"Same as always. You?"

"Hanging in there."

That would be the extent of our conversational interaction, but despite how restrained he was with me, my dad was great with the kids. He was full of stories from when he was growing up, which the kids loved hearing, and he was a master at recalling silly jokes.

Life for him and my mom had changed a couple of years ago, dementia slowly robbing my dad of his short-term memory and cognition. It had pained my mom, not being able to babysit the kids for me after Rebecca passed away, but she already had her hands full with Dad.

I sat down, and the kids piled in on either side of the table, laughing and hiccupping, my sister having chased them there, whooping and hollering to get them moving.

Taylor, Cindy, and Marcus.

Watching their animated, joyous faces gave me a moment of peace.

My mom was the last to sit down, only relenting with all her fussing when Sam started to fill his plate, murmuring about how hungry he was. Every food item she'd been preparing ended up on the table, serving dish protocol cast aside.

Once everyone was seated, the usual conversations about holiday plans for Christmas morning and New Year's Eve followed.

After a while, it was all too much. Any plans I'd been formulating in my mind for the holidays all revolved around spending time with Michael.

Without him, I was lost.

"Ryan." My mom reached across the table and touched my hand. "You've been quiet all evening. Are you not feeling well?"

I set my cutlery down, shaking my head. "Not really, no, Mom."

My dad's brow dipped. "Are you thinking about Rebecca?" Today seemed to be one of my dad's better days. He was following the conversation without any prompting from anyone.

"No, Dad." I used my napkin to wipe my mouth. "I mean, I do ...but that's not—" I dropped my napkin onto my plate. I couldn't eat any more.

"You've taken on a lot, all on your own, Ryan." My mom rose to her feet and started cleaning plates away. "Maybe you should consider asking that Amy from work out on a date."

"That's a good idea," Sam interjected, then annihilated another mouthful of food. His plate was a smear of turkey, mashed potatoes, brussel sprouts, stuffing, and cranberry sauce.

"You really should." Janice touched my arm. "We just want you to be happy."

I clenched my jaw to temper my level of irritation at the same record being played over and over again. I never should have mentioned Amy's interest in me to any of them.

"I appreciate your concern, but I'm not looking for a relationship."

My mom lifted my plate. "It's not good to be alone. You need someone in your life, someone you can come home to every day."

I turned in my chair to face her. "You don't think I know that ...or want that?"

"So, what's the problem?" My dad folded his arms across his chest.

I pushed my chair back, prepared to rise to my feet. "I'm not looking for a relationship because I was seeing someone recently

…and it ended badly."

"Oh, Ryan …you didn't." It was Janice, and her tone wasn't helpful. I hadn't done anything wrong. Michael and I were adults, and we'd entered into an adult relationship.

"Didn't what?" My mom's hand came to rest on the back of my neck as she re-entered the dining room. "What did you do, Ryan?"

"Nothing, Mom …" I pinched the bridge of my nose, but the brigade of tears regrouping couldn't be persuaded to stay put. Two thin streams of anguish spilled down my cheeks.

Cindy's little hand touched mine. "Daddy, are you all right?"

I turned to her, attempting to lift my lips into a convincing smile, but it likely appeared more like a tear-streaked grimace. There was no point in lying to her. All three kids were aware something was wrong. "No, sweetheart, Daddy isn't doing well."

"What happened, Ryan?" My mom sat back down in her seat, apron still on, tea towel in hand in case she needed to wipe her hands.

I leaned forward and covered my face with my hands. There was no way out of this. They were my family. They deserved to know. "I fell in love, Mom. That's what happened. I fell in love with someone who wasn't available …and they broke my heart."

"Oh, Ryan—" Janice whispered beside me.

I snapped my head up and glared at her. "Can you stop that, please. I'm sorry if you don't approve, but it's not really any of your business."

Taylor snickered and stabbed a piece of carrot. "I know who it is."

"Keep it to yourself, Taylor." Janice pursed her lips and turned her attention back to me. "I told you someone was going to get hurt."

"Well, good for you." I rose to my feet. "You were right."

"What am I missing?" Sam asked as the doorbell rang. "I didn't even know Ryan was seeing anyone." He pushed his seat back and headed for the front entry. "I'll get it."

I looked down at my phone. There weren't any messages …any missed calls.

Surely, he wouldn't.

I couldn't see the front door from where I was standing. The dining room was situated around the corner from the living room.

Once Sam opened the door, a hushed conversation ensued.

It can't be.

I wasn't sure I could handle seeing him.

I placed my hand on my chest, the rise and fall frantic and labored. I was having trouble breathing. Michael would have known where I'd be tonight, but he should have been moving his stuff into Brenda's house today. There was no reason for him to be here.

Please, no.

I can't.

Sam walked back toward the dining room, and cocked his thumb toward the door, looking puzzled. "It's Mikey, but he won't talk to me. He's here for you, Ryan. Something is wrong."

He's here for you.

Those words—the room closed in on me like a kaleidoscope, fractal shapes and colors changing the landscape beneath my feet.

I reached for the table to keep myself from losing my balance as the sound of Michael's anguished sobs—gasping and shuddering—spilled into the dining room.

He was having a complete nervous breakdown in my parents' front hall.

I'd never moved so fast.

My mom's whispered, "Stay here," to the rest of my family barely registered.

I had Michael wrapped up in my arms before I'd even had a chance to think. He was shaking as he clung to me, his hands seeking reassurance. "I couldn't do it, Ryan ...I couldn't."

"Couldn't do what?" I held Michael at arm's length so I could see his face. It was mottled and slick with tears. I'd never seen anyone look so distraught ...so lost.

"Brenda ..." Michael shook his head. "I couldn't do it."

"Okay." I took him back into my arms, rocking him.

"My kids ..." Michael buried his face in the folds of my sweater, gasping through each breath. I had to hold Michael upright as his knees nearly buckled beneath him. "I can't lose them."

"You won't, baby ...you won't," I whispered to him, frantic to know why Michael had changed his mind about moving in with Brenda. He'd been adamant he didn't have a choice.

I pulled him tight against me. "We'll figure it out."

Behind Michael, Sam was standing silently, watching us, a look of confusion on his face. He'd known Michael and I had been hanging out a lot, but I guess it hadn't occurred to him that we'd become close enough to engage in the desperate grip we had on each other.

I broke eye contact with my brother, concentrating on the pain radiating from the shattered man in my arms. For as long as Michael wanted me to hold him, I would.

He was breaking my heart all over again.

"Baby," I whispered into his ear. "Tell me what happened."

Michael glanced up at my brother, then back at me. "Can we go somewhere else to talk? Maybe outside. I have a bunch of presents for the kids in the car."

"Sure, yeah." I grabbed my coat from the rack in the front hall and headed out the door toward Michael's car. All the way down the driveway, we weren't able to break contact with one another.

Hands touching, shoulders bumping—our bodies so close, we were like two magnets that refused to be pulled apart now that we'd reconnected.

We arrived at Michael's car, and he pulled open one of the side doors. He hadn't been kidding. The back seat was full of presents.

Before he had a chance to retrieve them, Michael faltered, clinging to the frame of the open door. I touched his face, wiping the remnants of earlier tears from his cheeks.

"Talk to me."

Michael looked up at me. "I couldn't do it, Ryan. I couldn't move in with her."

"Why, Michael?" I pressed my forehead against Michael's, holding his face in both hands. "Why did you change your mind? You said you could make it work."

Michael locked his eyes onto mine, causing my soul to melt from the intensity. There was more emotion emanating from those eyes than I'd ever seen before.

"The last time we were together, Ryan …I noticed you weren't wearing your wedding ring." Michael brushed his thumb along my bottom lip. "I couldn't move in with Brenda, because I couldn't stop thinking about what that might mean." He ran his hand up into my hair, along my ear, then cupped my face. "Surely, you must know how much I love you."

My knees nearly betrayed me, words I'd never expected to hear echoing in my mind. I'd thought I was alone in my feelings. That I'd be forever denying them—burying them.

"I may need you to repeat that," I whispered.

Michael moved his hands onto my back, cradling me. "I love you, Ryan Middleton, and I don't care who knows it. You made me whole again." He brushed his lips against mine. "I'd lost my passion, then you came along and reminded me why I love music."

He kissed me, ever so softly, his breath capturing mine, reuniting us. I could feel the depth of his love flowing into me like a warm, melodic infusion.

As our lips parted, I realized I'd felt it before from him. That last night we were together when Michael had asked for my absolute presence. I'd felt it in the way he kissed me that night.

Michael hummed against my lips, his light returning.

I was consumed by it—submitting to it.

"You unhinge me, Michael." I played my fingers along his beard, cheekbone to chin. "From that very first day in the coffee shop, you awoke something in me."

Michael knew what was coming.

Fresh tears streaked down his cheeks, wetting his lips.

"I love you too," I whispered then dove headlong into a sensual kiss, a testimony of devotion I'd never experienced before. I propelled Michael backward against his car. I wanted to transfer these feelings into something much more physical.

Time and place.

I was reluctant to release him.

Michael took hold of my face, peppering my lips with quick snatches of contact. He released me. "I don't know what to say …" He shook his head. "We almost messed this up, so badly."

"That's behind us now."

"But my kids, Ryan …,"

"We'll figure it out, I promise." I hugged him to me, burying my face against his cheek, thrilling in the familiar sensation of his beard against my skin. "Together. We'll figure it out."

"I didn't know what else to do." Michael moved his hand to the back of my head, and sought my mouth, extinguishing any fears I had of ever losing him again.

I gasped for breath as he released me.

"I couldn't live without you, Ryan. I just couldn't …"

I hadn't heard him walking down the driveway, my brother, but he soon made his presence known. Sam's rough hands on the back of my coat hauling me away from Michael more than caught me off guard. I nearly slipped and fell on the ice when Sam shoved me.

"What the fuck, Ryan!" Sam took a step toward me, but Michael stepped in grabbing hold of Sam. He struggled out of Michael's grasp and pushed Michael back toward his car.

"What have you done?" Sam gathered himself up, prepared to come at me again. "You're sick, Ryan, you know that? How did you manage to suck Mikey into this twisted game of yours?"

"It's not a game, Sam."

"You did this …" Sam jabbed a finger at me, then pointed at Michael. "You did this to him."

"You have no idea what you're talking about." Michael slammed his car door. "I'm not a child anymore, Sam." He reached for me, taking my hand, and we headed for the house.

Sam stayed behind on the driveway, watching us, scowling—disgusted.

I'd expected that response from my little brother. He still saw *Mikey* when he looked at Michael, his kindergarten buddy. All I saw was the man I was in love with. My best friend, my lover— my partner. The person I wanted to spend the rest of my life with.

I hoped someday, Sam would come around.

Michael and I walked into the living room where everyone had gone back to what they were doing, except for Janice, who was hovering near the Christmas tree.

"Is everything all right?" Janice was the first to approach us. "I heard Sam yelling out there." She looked back and forth between Michael and me. "Please tell me this isn't what I think it is."

"Isn't what?" My mom wandered into the living room, my kids not far behind her.

"Uncle Mike," Cindy shrieked, leaping up and down as she ran toward us. "Sing some Christmas songs." She grabbed at Michael's sleeve, pulling at it. "Please …."

"Hold up a minute, all right." Michael reached down and scooped Marcus up, who'd been tugging at his pant leg. "Your dad and I are talking to Auntie and Grandma."

"Singing," Marcus whispered as his little arms wrapped around Michael's neck. Aside from myself, my youngest had been the one most upset by Michael's lack of presence.

"Soon." Michael settled a brief kiss on Marcus' unruly mop of hair. "I promise."

Those few actions alone would've sealed my decision.

Michael had become a part of my family.

"Mom …" I leaned into Michael and put my arm around his waist. "You remember Michael Sanderson." I looked up at him and placed my hand on his arm, my happiness only dampened by the uncertainty of how we were going to ensure Michael retained joint custody of his kids.

"The person you're in love with?" My mom put her hand over her mouth. Not out of disgust, but more out of wonderment. "The one you told us about."

Michael kissed the side of my head. "Yes, Mrs. Middleton.

That would be me."

Taylor exhaled an exasperated sigh and rolled his eyes. "It's about time." He fist-bumped Michael, then took off back to the table, taking advantage of the fact no one was keeping an eye on the whipped cream canister.

Michael nudged me, giving me a knowing glance. I grinned, delirious with love for him, unable to contain myself.

My exuberant joy must have caught my sister's eye.

"Oh, for fuck's sake ..." Janice reached for Michael and me and folded us into a long, drawn-out hug. "You're making my brother goofy happy, Michael ...welcome to the family."

I stood in the doorway, watching Michael as he tried to extract himself from his position on Cindy's bed, where he'd been reading her the third story of the night. It was a delicate dance not to wake her, and Michael was succeeding admirably.

"What time is it?" Michael whispered as he stepped out of her room into the hallway and pulled her door to an almost closed position. She liked it left open a crack.

I wrapped my arms around Michael's neck. "Merry Christmas time."

Michael's eyebrows rose. It had taken hours to calm the kids down once we'd brought them home from my parents'. The excitement of having Uncle Mike as their daddy's boyfriend in addition to Santa arriving soon had wound them up to freakish levels.

"Already? Wow." Michael nearly lifted me off my feet as he pulled me into his arms, crushing my body against him. His lips descended on mine, overthrowing any lingering anxiety I still had.

I knew without question; Michael was mine for good this time.

"Merry Christmas, baby." Michael held my face, his eyes enduing me with a love so strong, it caused me to sigh with exhilaration. He smiled at me. "Hang on to that feeling."

"Done." I stroked Michael's beard with my fingers. "I'll be in bed waiting for you."

"I'll only be a few minutes, promise." Michael's expression was pensive as he turned from me and headed downstairs to phone his dad. It was late, but Michael assured me his dad wouldn't mind. This was important. We needed his dad's help.

I rearranged myself in bed, struggling to concentrate on the book in my hands. I'd read the same passage eight times in the past twenty minutes. I was too distracted. Michael was taking longer than either of us had anticipated. Which was either a good thing or a horrible thing.

Michael finally stepped in through the door.

"Well …?" I sat up straighter in bed. The tugging smile on Michael's face before he lit up was all the answer I needed. I wanted to hear details, though. "What did he say about the kids?"

"You were right." Michael closed and locked the door. "Brenda doesn't have a case. My dad says we should pick Mandy and Michael Jr. up this afternoon in accordance with our original agreement. If she gives us any trouble, he says we should call him, and he'll deal with it."

"*We* should call him …" I flung back the covers to let Michael into bed. He'd stripped out of the uncharacteristically casual t-shirt and sweatpants he'd arrived in at my parents'.

"Yeah, I told him about you." Michael stroked my face, then took the book from my hand and flung it onto the floor. He climbed on top of me, straddling my hips, and kissed me. "I told him I've been seeing this incredible guy recently. And I've fallen in love with him."

"How did he take it?" I gasped out a sigh, not sure I cared. Michael's mouth was traveling from behind my ear to the front of my throat, sucking, biting—licking long lines along my skin.

"The part he was surprised about is that you're Sam's big brother."

"So, an age thing …not that I'm a guy." I brushed my hand through Michael's hair as his mouth swept down to my chest, his tongue tasting every inch of my skin.

Michael circled one of my nipples with his tongue, then pulled lightly on it with his teeth. He glanced up at me. "No, not really. They'd been wondering why I was so happy recently."

I dug my hands into Michael's hair, clutching him to me.

"And are you? Happy?"

Michael kissed the base of my throat. "Deliriously."

"Just checking." I released Michael and brushed my hands along his arms, soaking in the texture of his skin. I raised my arms above my head when Michael nudged me into submitting.

I slid further down in bed, Michael's hot breath tickling the hair under my arm, his tongue licking vast swaths of my skin, my temptation to squirm overridden by the aching response of my cock. I closed my eyes, riding through each wave of desire.

Michael slid his hands into mine, our fingers intertwining. The scent of my perspiration on his lips launched me into overdrive. I lunged up at his lips, wanting them to consume me. Needing to feel his tongue filling my mouth—needing to feel his love for me.

Needing to be filled by him.

"Michael," I whispered when Michael allowed me to breathe. "Please …"

"I will …" Michael kissed me. "But I have something I want to ask you first."

"Anything." I swept my lips across Michael's beard, and bit at his chin, rocking my hips up, reveling in the feel of our cocks sliding past one another.

"Anything?" Michael's lips were hot on me, disabling my ability to concentrate.

He knew I'd do anything for him. A whimpering cry left my lips as he latched onto the sensitive skin above my collarbone. I wrapped my legs around his hips, digging my fingers into the firm flesh of his ass.

Michael's heated breath reached my lips again.

"Would you marry me?"

My heart jumped in my chest. *Now, later ...someday?* I released Michael's ass and raked my fingers up into his hair. "Are you asking me now?"

Michael pulled back, gazing down at me, his emerald eyes glimmering with uncertainty. He licked his lips and furrowed his brow. "I think I might be."

I touched his face. "You're serious."

Michael's gorgeous eyes rimmed with tears as he nodded his head. "I am."

Three short months ago, I'd been desperately alone, grieving—mourning my Rebecca, not able to move forward. Then this caring, intelligent, light-hearted man had come into my life and thrown everything upside down. Michael had opened my heart to a love I'd never thought possible.

A love that was one of the purest experiences of my life.

A love that was destined.

A love seated in my soul.

I held Michael's face and kissed the man I knew to be my soul mate. It had taken us a while to find each other, but now we had, and neither of us had any reason to wait.

"Yes," I whispered against Michael's lips. "Forever, yes."

Dear Reader

If you enjoyed *Christmas Blues*, please consider leaving a review. Reviews and word of mouth are the best way for readers to find content they love and to make books more visible.

It really makes a big difference.

Happy Reading!

Leigh

About the Author

Leigh Jarrett (she/he) is an unabashedly queer, quirky, and passionate author of Contemporary MM+ Romantic Fiction. Their published contemporary works include warm and always sexy HEA romances as well as dark romances filled with grit, trauma, and angst.

In their hometown of Victoria, BC, Canada, Leigh can be found nestled up with their fabulously supportive wife and trusty laptop or enjoying the wondrous Vancouver Island outdoors.

Please consider subscribing to Leigh's newsletter to stay up to date with their new releases and promos. If you're interested in MM+ Fantasy and Paranormal Romance, check out one of Leigh's other pen names, JT Fader, on their JT Fader Fantasticals website and newsletter jtfader.com.

To connect with Leigh Jarrett:

Email: leigh@leighjarrett.com

Website and newsletter: leighjarrett.com

You can also find Leigh on Bluesky

Other Books by Leigh Jarrett

"It all came down to a matter of trust."
A Friends to Lovers M/M Gay Romance
Snowblind

"Find love in the least expected place."
An Enemies to Lovers M/M Gay Romance

Merlot Rebellion

"Risking it all to follow your heart."
A Found Family M/M Bisexual Romance

Capital Adoration

"Brave enough to pursue love."
An Age Gap M/M Gay Romance

Pacific Pursuit

"Learning a new path to love."
A Roommates to Lovers Bisexual Awakening M/M Romance

Academic Adoration

"Recovering true love."
A Second Chance Hurt/Comfort M/M Romance

Drag Undivided

"Strumming your way to love."
A Grumpy/Sunshine Gay Awakening M/M Romance

Rhythmic Bliss